WARPATH

J.H. MILLS

ENSŌ
STUDIOS

ISBN: 979-8-9987327-3-7

For Tricia, Tracey and Katherine.

ACKNOWLEDGMENTS

Thank you to:

My Editor, Fleetwood Robbins. Your guidance and expertise is second to none. Your mastery of the form helped me continue Countess's journey in the way I had always envisioned it.

James Paradies and Jennifer Plumley. Your friendship and support over the years has meant the world to me.

My colleagues at Vassar College, Your strength, wisdom and guidance encouraged me to finally start publishing my work. Thank you all.

Table of Contents

Introduction

Previously, in AETHER…

I n the wake of a one-day nuclear war—the **Day of Fire**—a secretive government agency called **PHOENIX** enacted its long-prepared contingency plan. Global elites and federal operatives retreated deep underground, launching **Neo-Columbia**—their vision for a reborn United States.

Seven centuries later, the Hudson Valley has become **Vorpal Vale**—a harsh, post-apocalyptic wilderness where radiation lingers, crops fail, and mutated creatures prowl the ruins of old America. Humanity is divided into two fractured kingdoms, **Yorke** and **Saug**, locked in a simmering war that has lasted for two decades.

In the Kingdom of Yorke, **Countess Ella Wellington**, recently retired from intelligence service, is reluctantly pulled back into duty. Meanwhile, in a neighboring spiritual enclave, **Umbra Priestess Vilma**, devout follower of the deity **Sky Mother**, defies her elders and embarks on a perilous quest to retrieve the legendary **Rings of Callifrey**, said to be an ancient weapon of terrible power.

As their journeys intertwine, a subtle manipulator watches from behind the curtain: **Holly**, a charming, childlike entity who speaks through the eyes of a robotic doll. Though she appears friendly, Holly is executing a secret and sinister agenda through PHOENIX's long-abandoned infrastructure—and she may be the only one who remembers how the world truly ended.

Their paths converge at **Aether Storm**, an ancient research facility turned battlefield. There, Priestess is captured, her companions slain. Countess returns home with the Rings of Callifrey—and the crushing revelation that she, Priestess, and everyone around them are not human at all.

They are **Operarius**: artificial bodies housing preserved human brains, harvested by PHOENIX centuries ago.

Now Countess must wrestle with the truth of her own identity:

If your memories are real but your body is not, what does it mean to be human?

Prologue

One week later…

Basement Level — Greystone Barony

Priestess had been in the prison cell for several days. It was small. Sterile but not clean. The dark stone walls thrummed with hidden machinery, and every hour metallic chimes rang through the vents—like a monastery bell marking time in a godless temple.

She had plenty of time to think. She'd wept for the entire first day.

Losing Sobun felt like losing a lung—an organ torn from her. And Ansel… his loss weighed heavy too. They had been so different. So noble in their own ways. Now both were gone, and all she had left were memories and fury.

She'd stopped praying on the second day. Whatever gods had survived the Day of Fire weren't listening.

When Holly appeared outside the cell, Priestess stood.

"How are you doing?" Holly asked sweetly. "Staff treating you well?"

Priestess looked away. "Fuck off, devil doll."

"Oh, don't be mad. You should be happy. Countess didn't kill you."

"You lied to me."

"I lie to everyone," Holly said, matter-of-fact. "It was necessary. Not malicious. One day you'll understand."

"I trusted you. I followed your instructions. You led me into a trap, and now the people I care about are dead."

"Were they close?" Holly asked, feigning curiosity. "Admit it—you barely knew them."

"I got to know them," Priestess snapped. "They were good men. They deserved better."

"You all do."

Priestess gripped the bars. "And yet, here I am. In a cage."

"That's why I'm here." Holly smiled faintly. "I want to offer you a job."

Priestess raised a brow. "What's the catch?"

"Join Countess. Join her team."

Priestess laughed coldly. "Tell her to choke on a circuit board."

Holly folded her arms, waiting.

"No way," Priestess growled. "She attacked me. Killed my team. She can die in a fire."

"What if I told you... it was my fault?"

Priestess narrowed her eyes. "And why would you be helping her?"

"I need a team," Holly said simply.

"You had two good ones," Priestess spat. "Now you've got one broken team... and one pissed-off priestess."

"I'm hoping to build something better—after you've had some rest."

"And if I say no?"

"Then, unfortunately... you don't leave this cell."

Priestess stared at her. "Let's say I say yes. What's the mission?"

"Iroquois Warpath," Holly said.

Priestess mouthed the words. "That's... two nouns. What is an Iroquois Warpath?"

"It's a PHOENIX facility. Like Eternal Taiga. Like Aether Storm. But worse. High-security and exceptionally lethal."

Priestess crossed her arms. "And what's inside that's so important?"

Holly leaned in, almost conspiratorial. "Information."

"Vague," Priestess said.

"Vital," Holly countered. "It may help save this dying planet."

Priestess exhaled, slow. "Fine," she said at last. "I'll work with Countess. Not for her. Just... toward survival."

Holly smiled. "Good. I'll have food sent to your cell, and we'll move you to better accommodations soon. You'll still be here a bit longer, though. Sorry about that."

Priestess threw up her hands. "No problem!"

"You look tired," Holly said softly. "You should lie down."

Priestess froze. Her pupils dilated, breath catching. Slowly, mechanically, she turned and walked to the cot.

"We are such stuff as dreams are made on," she murmured, her voice flattening.

"And our little life," Holly replied, "is rounded with a sleep."

Priestess lay down. Closed her eyes. Fell still.

Holly smiled, almost tender. "That's a good girl."

Then she flickered—like a candle in the wind—and blinked out, leaving the godless temple just a shade darker than before.

Act I
Strike Force

1

The drones fell like black rain, and Countess moved like a shadow through the broken urban landscape. Her rifle bucked against her shoulder. Waves of attacking machines pressed hard, relentless. Lin covered the gaps in formation with clean, surgical fire. Around them, the mechanical horde reeled under the onslaught.

"Left flank—clear!" Lin called.

"Push the center!" Countess ordered.

They advanced, hammering the enemy back, meter by bloody meter. Drones shattered under the hail of bullets, mechanical bodies sparking and writhing as they fell. For a brief, heady moment, victory felt possible—as if all the training, all the pain, might actually lead to a win.

The enemy lines buckled.

Stitch whooped in triumph. "We got 'em on the ropes!"

Then the sky changed.

Without warning, the amber-tinted sun flickered,

dimming to a cold steel gray.

A smooth voice—neutral, polite, utterly devoid of emotion—rolled across the battlefield:

"Phase Two: Adaptation."

Countess barely had time to register the words before the ground beneath their boots shifted—literally. Barricades retracted. New drone portals opened like wounds in the earth.

From them poured heavier warforms: titanium-plated battle mechs, stealth drones, agile quadrupeds with gleaming plasma weaponry.

Their HUDs exploded in a blizzard of threat indicators.

"Fall back! Regroup on me!" Countess snapped, instincts kicking in.

Lin was already pivoting toward her—but Stitch, drunk on the earlier momentum, bolted toward the nearest mech, weapon blazing.

"Stitch! Get back here!" Lin barked.

It was too late.

A mortar impacted near Stitch's position, tossing him end over end like a rag doll.

The squad's formation crumbled under the overwhelming surge.

Countess fought like a woman possessed, her rifle spitting defiance. Lin shouted something she couldn't hear over the rising crescendo of machine fury.

The black rain became a monsoon.

One by one, their vitals winked out.

Countess was the last to fall—a plasma blast ripping through her chest in a searing instant.

Her vision collapsed to black—and then orange capital letters burned across the darkness:

SIMULATION TERMINATED

The sim pod hissed open, flooding her with harsh white light and the antiseptic tang of ozone. Countess ripped off her helmet and staggered upright, soaked in sweat and trembling with frustration.

Across from her, Lin's helmet hit the deck with a clatter. His face was a thunderhead of rage.

"What the hell was that, Stitch?" he demanded.

Stitch climbed out of his pod. "I—I had an idea. Thought I saw an opening—"

"You thought wrong," Lin snapped, voice low and dangerous. "You broke formation. You disobeyed a direct order. Stick with the fucking plan!"

Countess wiped her face with the back of her glove, breathing hard.

"We don't beat them with ideas," she said, voice sharp

as a blade. "We beat them with discipline."

For a moment, none of them spoke.

The simulation bay buzzed with the muted chaos of other squads resetting—victors exulting, losers slumping in defeat. The air smelled of ozone, oil, and human sweat.

Then, without warning, their HUDs flickered to life once more.

Holly's bright, innocent doll face appeared, floating in the corner of their vision. Her voice—impossibly kind after the brutality they had just endured—filled their ears.

"I know it feels impossible right now," Holly said, smiling warmly. "But every obstacle has a solution. Iroquois Warpath isn't unconquerable. We'll find the way… together."

Countess closed her eyes for a beat, letting the words cool the fire inside her.

Holly's smile widened—just a little too wide.

With a soft plink, Holly's avatar vanished.

Countess stared at the empty air a moment longer than necessary.

Then, under her breath:

"Yeah. Together." But deep inside, unease gnawed at her.

Countess took a steadying breath and turned toward Stitch. She unclenched her jaw before speaking; the taste of copper lingered on her tongue.

"Walk with me," she said quietly.

He hesitated, glancing toward Lin—whose expression promised blood if he made another mistake—then followed her a few steps away from the sim pods. They stood near one of the deactivated combat dummies, its lifeless sensors staring past them like a silent witness.

Countess folded her arms, fixing him with a look colder than any shout.

"Holly just added you to the team, and she assures me you're good at what you do."

"Yes, but—" Stitch began.

"I know you're trying to make a good first impression," Countess continued, "and I know you want to prove you belong."

Stitch shifted awkwardly, his fingers twitching at his sides.

"But out there, your instincts don't matter if they aren't in step with the team. One bad choice doesn't just cost you. It costs all of us."

He nodded miserably, looking at the floor.

Countess leaned in slightly, voice low but cutting.

"You had an idea. Good for you. Next time—have it before the fight. Not during."

Stitch swallowed hard.

"Freelancing is bad. You don't go off on your own during a tactical situation."

He nodded. "Understood."

"Go think about it," she said, stepping back. "You're dismissed for the day."

Stitch gave a small, choked nod and started to walk away, shoulders hunched.

Behind them, Lin cupped his hands around his mouth and yelled after him:

"Sort your shit out!"

Nearby, several members of another squad chuckled under their breath. But Countess didn't crack a smile. She just watched Stitch go, wondering—not for the first time—how many more fights like this they could afford to lose.

Countess closed her eyes. Just for a breath—just long enough to slip.

The darkness behind her eyelids pulsed. Not from fatigue. Not from battle.

A flicker of light—red taillights cutting through heavy rain.

The sharp squeal of tires.

Glass breaking. Screams. A child's voice.

The smell of burnt sugar and plastic.

An emergency-room ceiling, swimming above her.

A cold mask pressed over her face. Rubber. The pain of a breathing tube forced down her throat.

A man's voice, cold and certain, came drifting up through memory:

"Both daughters. Initiate ASPHODEL."

Countess gasped.

Her eyes flew open. Her pulse was hammering. She was still in the sim bay. Lin was in front of her, staring into her eyes, his hands on her shoulders, steadying her.

"Hey. Are you okay?" he asked, voice low.

She hesitated a beat, then nodded once.

"Yeah," she said. "We're done here. You and Stitch— get some rest. We'll regroup tomorrow."

As the others turned to go, she stayed where she was, just for a moment longer.

Her hand clenched, hard, against her leg.

Asphodel…

The word echoed like a bone-deep shiver.

The black rain was only beginning.

2

D arius "Stitch" Korrin couldn't sit still. The barracks light was dim and sour, casting long shadows across the bunks. His gear was half-stowed, boots kicked off at uneven angles. A field-ration packet sat unopened on the table.

The ache in his reconstructed shoulder flared whenever he moved too fast—a souvenir from Holly's test program, the one he'd barely survived. The rest of his team hadn't been so lucky.

He paced. Then sat. Then stood again.

You had an idea. Next time—have it before the fight.

Countess's words looped in his head, as sharp and clean as the look she gave him. Not angry. Not disappointed. Just cold. Exacting.

He ran both hands through his hair, exhaling sharply.

It wasn't supposed to go like that.

He used to be good at this.

No—he was good at this.

Before he was recruited into Countess's team—back when the world still made sense—he wore a different uniform. Intelligence Corps. Surveillance Ops. Signals Branch. Intercept and manipulate.

In Intel, the people at the top didn't want soldiers. They wanted problem-solvers. And he was that. He'd always seen problems as machines—take them apart, find the flaw, rebuild them better.

"You're not here to follow rules," his old CO once told him.

"You're here to bend them until they snap the enemy in half."

He remembered that day like it was painted in firelight:

A routine observation post—two agents tracing a rogue signal near the northern wall.

Everything jammed. Protocol said wait for clearance.

He didn't wait.

Stitch rerouted the signal through a mesh of abandoned surveillance towers, guessed the frequency distortion pattern, and launched a trace—caught the mole in under ninety seconds.

They called it "initiative."

They called him "essential."

They gave him a promotion, a raise, a higher clearance level.

So why the hell did that instinct just get him chewed out by Countess?

When did the rules change?

He sat down hard on the edge of his bunk, elbows on his knees, staring at the scuffed floor.

The sim. The battle. He thought he saw an opening. He did see one. But the moment he broke formation, the whole thing came apart like wet paper.

Lin had practically bitten his head off.

Countess didn't even yell. That was worse—just precision disappointment.

He let out a quiet, bitter laugh.

"Hell of a first impression."

Across from his bunk, a small screen flickered. TacCom drills queued and waiting.

He tapped one. It displayed tight formations, call-and-response orders, team sweeps.

Boring. Rigid. Predictable.

But it worked.

He scrubbed a hand down his face and leaned forward. Tapped another drill. Then another. He let it play.

Hold formation. Line sweep. Advance on beat. Tight pattern. Recenter. Recenter.

The language felt foreign.

He opened a new file. Started typing.

Stitch—Tactical Note to Self

NO SOLO PLAYS

INSTINCT ≠ DISCIPLINE

CUNNING ≠ COHESION

YOU'RE NOT IN YORKE INTEL ANYMORE

He stared at the words for a long moment.

Then added one more line.

FALL IN LINE. TRUST MUST BE EARNED.

He saved the file. Closed the screen.

Still no appetite. Still no boots on.

But for the first time all night, Stitch sat still.

3

Countess sat alone in the dark. The dorm's overhead lights were off, reduced to a faint ambient strip running along the ceiling's edge. She hadn't moved since returning. Her jacket lay in a crumpled pile near the door. Her helmet still sat in her lap.

Her hands trembled.

She'd told Lin she was fine. Told Stitch to get rest. But now she couldn't remember how to breathe.

The sim was just training. They all knew that. But something about it—the black rain, the voice, the sudden collapse—had cracked something loose inside her.

She pressed her palms to her temples, squeezing as though she could hold her thoughts in place.

But the memory was already moving. Slow. Inevitable.

Like a crash you couldn't stop.

Countess thought about Vance. She'd lost teammates before, but Vance was different. She'd only known him for a short time, yet the days had felt compressed somehow—each one stretched thin, carrying the weight of years.

Poor Vance. Priestess's strong man, Sobun, had nearly cleaved him in two. But without Vance's sacrifice, Lin wouldn't be alive. She felt guilty for even appreciating that Lin had survived. He was the better soldier, after all. But both of them owed their lives to Vance.

She honored him the only way she knew—with silence. A few moments in the dark, a quiet place in her mind. Then, at last, she let him go.

Her fingers brushed the helmet in her lap. Cold metal. The same kind they used in the hospital.

* * *

Rain.

She was in the back seat. The world outside was slick and gray, blurred headlights dragging across the windshield. Her mother's voice cut through the sound of the wipers.

"No, I'm not signing anything until I speak with him directly."

A pause. Frustrated silence. Her mother hung up.

In the front seat, her older sister crossed her arms.

"Nice," she muttered. "Now he's definitely not coming."

Her mother didn't respond. Just drove faster.

The taillights ahead turned yellow, then red.

The brakes screeched.

The world turned sideways.

* * *

Light.

Glass exploded. Screams. Metal folding. Heat.

She was weightless, then too heavy.

Then nothing.

* * *

Ceiling.

Flashing red strobes overhead. Movement. Cold air. Plastic masks.

A logo with wings. ARCH…something? ARCHANGEL.

She was strapped to a gurney, still half in her ruined dress, her hands scraped and bloody.

Someone was shouting.

"She's tachy! Where's the other one?"

"Unresponsive. Pulse erratic. We need to intubate!"

"I've got the younger stabilized. Barely."

Machines beeped. Doors hissed open.

Two figures entered—their voices calm amid the chaos.

Vanessa Caldwell's voice cut through the noise like a scalpel.

"Everyone breathe. We're not here to interfere. We're here to facilitate."

Countess turned her head. Just enough to glimpse the woman.

She was tall, precise, immaculately dressed in crimson heels and a deep blue coat, her dark hair swept perfectly back, framing green eyes that missed nothing.

Her tone was soothing. Rehearsed. Powerful.

Behind her stood a man built like a soldier, posture sharp and unmoving. Shaved head. Thick forearms crossed beneath a high-collared black coat.

"That's Spencer Mackey," someone whispered. "They call him Janus."

Countess couldn't see his eyes—only the rigid authority of his presence.

Vanessa scanned the room, eyes settling on the lead trauma surgeon.

"Doctor, I need both patients cleared for specialist handoff. Now."

The surgeon shook his head. "They're in critical condition. I can't guarantee either will survive a conventional procedure—let alone a field transfer."

"You won't need to," said Janus—his voice low, iron and smoke.

"She's already a candidate. So is the sister. We've seen their records. Their father's work... requires continuity."

"You served with him, didn't you?" Vanessa asked.

"I did," Janus replied. "In Kandahar."

"And?" she prompted.

"I owe him this."

The word came softly, like a death sentence:

"Initiate the ASPHODEL protocol."

Gasps. One nurse took a step back.

"We're not authorized. We'd need—"

"You have it," Janus said. "Authorization approved."

Vanessa turned to him, her voice soft but loaded.

"What do we tell him?"

He didn't answer.

Vanessa blinked once, then nodded.

"Right. They died together—too far gone. It'll play."

She turned back to the stunned staff, flashing a public-relations smile that didn't reach her eyes.

"Let's do this quickly. Dignity, people."

* * *

The walls changed.

They were moving her now—her gurney gliding through a polished corridor, past signs that read RESTRICTED and ETERNAL TAIGA.

She passed beneath a glowing symbol she didn't recognize.

It looked like a flower. Or a circle of thorns.

ASPHODEL.

The chamber was cold. Silent. Like a church where no one came to pray.

Steel arches rose into an inky black dome above.

Candlelight flickered beneath antiseptic surgical rigs. Data slates hummed alongside old-world incense burners.

People moved in crimson-trimmed robes—PHOENIX technicians, but they didn't speak like medical staff. They spoke like clerics.

"The host shall sleep."

"The mind glorified."

"All hail Columbia."

"Columbia shall rise."

A priest drew a symbol on her forehead with a gloved finger. Not quite a cross. Not quite a circuit.

Across from her, her sister was already sedated. Her eyes fluttered open—just for a second.

They locked eyes.

Don't forget me. Please...

The priest whispered, "Two with matching genelines. Exceptional."

Another voice said, "These are gifts. Father-given."

Countess tried to speak, but a mask descended over her mouth.

Rubber. Sterile.

A sour taste. A burning in her lungs.

She felt the cold steel of the table beneath her. The light above turned amber.

A screen blinked:

SUBJECT ACCEPTED

GENOMIC MATCH: 99.9%

ANESTHETIC: APPLIED

ASPHODEL PROCESS – BEGIN

The last thing she saw was the PHOENIX seal, glowing red and gold above the surgical archway.

Then a voice, soft as winter frost:

"Close your eyes now, little one.

You won't remember any of this.

But you will be remembered… until Columbia calls for you."

* * *

She woke with a start.

The dorm was silent.

Countess sat up slowly, hands curled into fists. Her undershirt clung to her back, damp with sweat.

The HUD superimposed onto her field of vision flickered. She acknowledged a notice as her pulse began to settle.

But the anxiety stayed. She stared at the far wall, at nothing.

"They didn't save us," she whispered.

"They stored us."

4

The warehouse hummed with late-night energy: drones flashing past on rails, heavy loaders shifting crates, the mechanical pulse of the kingdom's hidden war machine.

Countess leaned against a cold steel column, arms folded, watching the elevator bank across the way.

The dining deck had emptied hours ago. Lin and Stitch were off somewhere, blowing off steam — sanctioned downtime after another long session in the sims.

It was just her now. Waiting.

The elevator chimed, and a figure stepped out.

Slim, upright, dark hair braided tightly down her back. Gray uniform jacket.

Eyes like sharpened glass.

Priestess.

Holly walked beside her in projection form, looking almost sheepish.

"I thought it best if I introduced you," Holly said brightly — almost like a mother embarrassed to make two kids play together.

Countess straightened. Priestess met her gaze without flinching.

"Countess, meet your new teammate," Holly said. "Priestess, this is your unit lead. Play nice, you two."

There was the faintest shimmer of amusement under Holly's polished tone, but it vanished as quickly as it appeared.

Without waiting for a reply, Holly's avatar flickered and blinked out of sight.

The silence that followed was thick enough to chew.

Countess pushed off the pillar and approached. She extended a hand.

Priestess hesitated — not for long, but enough.

When she finally shook it, her grip was steady, strong — but cold.

"Welcome to the team," Countess said.

Priestess gave a slight nod. No smile.

They found a quiet corner of the dining deck, half in

shadow, the low thrum of distant machinery filling the gaps between words.

Countess sat first, motioning for Priestess to do the same. The other woman remained standing for a moment before sitting opposite her, posture rigid.

"Look," Countess said, keeping her voice calm. "I know you didn't choose this. None of us—"

"You killed my team," Priestess said. Her eyes were daggers. "Two good men. Great men."

She tilted her head slightly, studying Countess the way one might study a new weapon — looking for cracks.

"Yes," Countess said evenly. "And Holly wanted me to kill you, too. Did she tell you that?"

"No. But—" Priestess faltered, uncertain why.

"It's true," said Countess. "We both lost in Holly's stupid game. Let's agree to put that behind us. It happened. We were both put in situations we didn't control or understand."

"Yes," Priestess admitted. She nodded softly and looked away.

"But we're really in it now," Countess continued. "This strike force we're preparing for is deadly serious. I need a unit that moves as one. No lone operators. No second agendas."

A flicker passed across Priestess's face — quick and bitter.

"I'm not looking to undermine you," she said, clipped. "I

don't have time for politics."

"Good," Countess said. "I know you're strong — an excellent leader. But there's only room for one team lead. However..." — she let the word hang — "there is room for a second-in-command. When you're ready."

Another long silence.

Priestess looked away, watching a service drone roll past hauling a tray of empty mugs.

"Maybe you'll earn my trust," she said finally, voice low.

"Maybe you'll earn mine," Countess replied.

For the first time, a faint, almost imperceptible smile ghosted the corner of Priestess's mouth. It was gone in an instant.

* * *

The conversation drifted—naturally, cautiously—to broader things.

"What do you think happens," Priestess asked after a while, "if someone refuses Strike Force duty?"

Countess leaned back, feeling the cold of the metal seat seep through her shirt.
"I don't know," she said honestly. "Nobody talks to me about it."

"There are rumors," Priestess said. "That they disappear. Executed."

Countess shook her head. "That hasn't been my experience. I think Holly... recycles them."

Priestess frowned. "Recycles?"

"She wipes their short-term memory," Countess explained. "Gives them another job. A safe job, out of the fight. My head of housekeeping, Mrs. Baybridge, was one of them. Supremely capable... but she just decided she'd had enough."

Priestess's mouth twisted. "Better than a bullet. Or a sword to the back."

"Maybe," Countess said. "Depends on what you think living really means."

The warehouse beyond them thrummed with a steady, mechanical heartbeat.

* * *

The corridor was dim, quiet — one of the older transit shafts sealed off during duty hours. Overhead, a single flickering panel hummed like a trapped insect.

Countess and Priestess walked side by side, their boots striking the metal in quiet rhythm. Neither had spoken since the sim bay.

"I used to think this whole thing was just Phoenix flexing," Priestess said, her tone more thoughtful than bitter. "One more monument to themselves. 'Look how many corpses we can stack to win a war they started.'"

"You don't think that anymore?" Countess asked.

"No," Priestess said. "Now I think they're scared. Where are they? They all ran away somewhere. They refuse to show themselves. And that makes them worse."

"Except for Holly."

"Yeah, about that…" Priestess glanced at her. "Holly doesn't strike me as really being part of Phoenix."

"No?"

"No. Well… maybe. She seems like an outsider somehow. Everything I've seen of Phoenix is regimented. Precise. Holy, even. Like their plans are based on divine scripture."

Countess laughed under her breath. "I know what you mean. It's all so over-the-top."

"Holly?" Priestess said. "She's all pink hair and pep talks."

"And speaking of Phoenix," Countess added, "got any theories on where they went?"

Priestess didn't hesitate. "I think they blew themselves up during the Day of Fire. And good riddance."

"All of them? No." Countess shook her head. "They have to be out there. Somewhere. Waiting…"

They walked a few more steps in silence. Countess watched Priestess from the corner of her eye.

"You and I were in the same Holly loop for hundreds of years," she said. "Fighting and dying. Fighting and surviving."

Priestess nodded. "Yeah. What do you think is really going on here? What's Holly trying to do?"

"I think Holly's got a plan to save the world. Although she's not sharing the specifics—"

"You really buy that shit?"

Countess hesitated. "Yes, but… I take your point. She's lied to us before."

"Damn right she has. Seems like lies are all that comes out of her god-forsaken mouth."

"And yet we're still stuck doing her bidding," Countess said. "Quit, and we're back in the training loop… or worse."

"Yeah," Priestess muttered. "No choice. We do the thing at Iroquois Warpath… or die trying."

"You ever think we've done this before?" Priestess asked suddenly.

Countess stopped mid-step. "What do you mean?"

"I mean… what if this isn't our first Strike Force? What if this is our fifth—or fiftieth? Every time it fails, she just resets the board."

Countess frowned. "We know this isn't the first Strike Force. Holly said she's been trying to get in for a long time."

"No, not that," Priestess said. "I mean what if *we've* been here before... and we failed. What if this is our hundredth time? Our thousandth?"

"Wipe the files," Countess murmured. "Recycle the assets."

"Exactly. She could just scoop our brain jar off the floor and shove it into a new body."

Countess winced. "That's a horrifying thought. But I don't think it's that simple."

She paused, lowering her voice.

"...I had a flashback today," she said quietly. "A *real* memory. Not sim data."

Priestess glanced over, suddenly focused. "Think so? Are you sure? What kind of memory?"

"It felt real. Vivid. There was a car crash. A hospital. And a name."

Countess hesitated. Then said it.

"Asphodel."

Priestess stopped cold.

"I know that name," she said slowly. "But from where?"

Countess shook her head. "I don't know. I can't quite place it. Somewhere old."

They reached the end of the corridor. Just as they turned, a soft plink chimed in their HUDs.

[TACCOM: HOLLY] Reminder: Debrief begins in fifteen minutes. You've got this! Eyes up, hearts strong!

Priestess looked at Countess, deadpan.

"She says it like she means it."

Countess didn't smile.

"That's what scares me."

* * *

"Report for duty tomorrow," Countess said.

Priestess nodded once. As she turned to leave, Countess called after her.

"I meant what I said... about second-in-command. Lin is an effective soldier, but he's not a leader. I need an alternate—someone I can trust."

Priestess paused, one hand on the rail leading toward the dormitory deck.

"I know," she said. And this time, the words carried just the faintest trace of something more than duty.

Then she turned and was gone, swallowed by the hum and haze of the Connector's endless twilight.

Countess stood alone a while longer, listening to the sound of machines preparing for a war they didn't even know they were fighting.

And somewhere, beneath the surface of things, the clock was ticking.

5

The Highpoint Connector loomed around them, a honeycomb of steel and reinforced concrete buried deep under the ancient foundations of Greystone Barony. It was Intelligence headquarters for Yorke Kingdom—the mind of the war with Saug Kingdom, if not the heart.

During the morning sim practice, Holly had contacted Countess's team.

"Take a breather," she said. "There's a full-team meeting in the Briefing Hall. One hour. And please—"

Her voice dropped to a mischievous, almost conspiratorial whisper:

"Come hungry for answers."

* * *

Countess tightened the straps of her field jacket as the special elevator hummed upward, carrying her and the team toward the Administration Level. The overhead lights buzzed in their metal sockets, casting everyone in a sterile blue-white glow.

Lin shifted next to her, silent. Stitch fidgeted with the strap on his gear bag, casting furtive glances at the walls as if they might close in.

The doors opened with a hydraulic sigh.

Before them stretched the Briefing Theater—a wide, tiered room filled with rows of steel benches and curved desks. About forty-five operatives already milled about, some in small clusters, others sprawled lazily across seats, laughing, trading inside jokes.

None of them turned to greet the newcomers.

Countess led her team down a side aisle, feeling the weight of eyes that weren't looking at them. An absence more pointed than any stare.

She caught flashes of insignia—Teams 1 through 9— sewn proudly onto jackets and sleeves. The old guard. The veterans.

And here we are, she thought. The expendables.

A woman jogged up to Countess, almost unnoticed.

"You're the new team, right?" she said.

"Oh!" said Countess. She really had been startled, but feigned playful overacting. "I guess so, yes. What can we do for you?"

"Here," said the woman. She thrust something into Countess's hand. "Sew them on at your earliest convenience." Then she jogged off.

Countess looked down at the small stack in her hand. Round clothing patches about the size of a drink coaster. Each had a black border and a prominent red 10 at the center. Team 10.

They found seats near the back. No one offered a space closer to the front.

The lights dimmed, and Holly's voice echoed over the hall's speaker system, impossibly cheerful.

"Good morning, Strike Force. Welcome to your final operational briefing. Apologies to those of you who are joining late. Countess, can you and your team stand up, please?"

Countess, Lin, Priestess, and Stitch all stood to silence and blank stares.

"Please welcome Team 10."

There was a momentary, weak, and scattered applause, then Countess's team sat again.

A holographic display shimmered to life at center stage, projecting a slowly rotating model of the Iroquois Warpath facility—an ugly steel screw buried in the countryside.

Holly's doll-faced avatar appeared, beaming down at them.

"The world is dying," she began, her voice losing none of its manufactured sweetness. "Crops are failing. Despite centuries of recovery after the Day of Fire, pockets of radiation remain. Mutation rates in plants and animals are still alarmingly high. But hope remains! Hidden within the Iroquois Warpath facility are technologies capable of restoring the environment, ending the famine, and giving humanity a second chance."

Murmurs ran through the crowd.

Countess exchanged a glance with Lin, who shrugged almost imperceptibly.

"It will not be easy," Holly continued. "Security at Iroquois Warpath is the most advanced we've ever seen. But that is why you are here. You are the best of the best. And together, we will succeed."

The hologram shifted to show a countdown timer: 13 days, 22 hours, 17 minutes.

"You have two weeks to finalize your preparations. Practice in simulation. Gather weapons and gear. General orders: use your judgment, but it is recommended you bring heavy firepower. Be careful with explosives. The security sector of Iroquois Warpath is filled with tight spaces—collateral damage is likely. Grenades are usually fine, but larger charges can accidentally kill your teammates."

The crowd chuckled darkly.

"And now," Holly said, "I would d like to introduce our field leaders."

Two men stepped forward onto the platform, one on each side. Twelve additional teammates, six on each side, took the stage behind them and stood at parade rest.

All of them wore dark gray flight suits; the leaders retained their standard sidearms and blades and wore maroon berets.

The first was tall and broad-shouldered, with the insignia of Team 1 on his left shoulder. His dark hair was buzzed tight against his scalp, his expression radiating a calm confidence. On his lower back, mounted horizontally, was a short sword.

"Commander Steve Stone," Holly announced.

The second man, slightly shorter but just as imposing, gave a lazy salute. His left shoulder bore the mark of Team 2. On his back, crossed with the handles sticking up over his shoulders, were two jungle machetes.

"And Captain Steve Church."

Stone took the podium, nodding once to the assembled teams.

"I won't go over the raid plan today because we've all seen it a hundred times. And all of your teams have been given extensive documentation. Learn it, know it. In two weeks, we'll have a final briefing with all the details."

Stone took a moment to scan the faces in the audience.

"We've all trained, fought, and bled for this. You know the drill—precision, communication, trust. Together we live. Separate, uncoordinated... we die. Every past attempt at Iroquois Warpath failed because teams fractured under pressure. That will not happen again. Now—questions?"

Countess stood immediately.

"I've read all the literature, and I have some ideas on how we might—"

"Thank you... Countess from Team Ten," said Stone. He smiled, but Countess could tell he felt she was talking out of turn. "I appreciate your enthusiasm. Come see me at some point after the briefing, and I'll be happy to hear your ideas."

Countess glanced across the stage to Steve Church. He was staring at her, furious.

"Now," said Stone, "I'm going to let Steve Church tell you about the most important tech we'll be using in the field: TacCom."

Stone took a step back from his podium, and Church walked to the podium on his side.

"Thank you, sir. For the benefit of our newer members," he said, glancing directly—and only briefly—

toward Countess's row, "we'll be reviewing the Tactical Command System."

He tapped a small remote, and the hologram shifted, revealing a glowing, three-dimensional schematic of the Rayon-Theta TacCom network.

"The TacCom system integrates seamlessly with the Operarius platform," Church said, voice crisp. "Providing full-spectrum battlefield control: air, ground, and maritime targeting, obstacle avoidance, positive ID at range, real-time threat prioritization."

He rattled off specifications—256-core CPU backbone, situational awareness in degraded environments, five-kilometer target acquisition—with the precision of a man reciting scripture.

"It's not a piece of equipment you need to carry with you. Each of you has it built in. Once you joined the Strike Force, Holly activated it inside you."

Church walked across the stage, his hands clasped behind his back.

"Congratulations, you now possess one of the finest command-and-control systems ever devised. Train with it until it's second nature. It will save your life at Iroquois Warpath. And if you can't keep up, TacCom will know before I do."

Countess listened, absorbing it all. Lin leaned forward slightly, interested despite himself. Even Stitch seemed momentarily awed.

Stone took over again, his tone more casual but no less certain.

"Our plan is simple: overwhelming force, coordinated strikes, hammer every door and crush every defense. We've reviewed all prior attempts, and this is the best model we've got."

He smiled.

"And for our newer teams... especially Team 10... study the video footage. Train hard. Stick to the plan."

Church leaned in. "...and don't do anything stupid."

Stone looked meaningfully at Church and cleared his throat.

"Sorry, sir," said Church. Countess enjoyed seeing Church get a small dressing-down, but she could tell he resented it.

Countess felt her jaw tighten. She liked Stone well enough, but Church seemed dangerous.

The briefing ended with a quick dismissal. Teams rose, clustered, buzzed with excitement or grim resolve.

* * *

When the briefing hall had thinned somewhat, Steve Church made a beeline for Countess.

"Hey, new girl," said Church.

"I'm sorry?" said Countess. "I'm a Countess and Lieutenant Commander in His Majesty's Intel—"

"Not anymore," interrupted Church. "Those titles don't mean shit here. And you Intel pukes are all the same with your secret codes and your passwords. You wouldn't last two seconds in the regular army."

"Is that—" Countess started.

"Shut up and listen. Because your life depends on it."

Lin had heard enough. He moved to get in Church's face, but two members of Church's team grabbed him by the arms.

Priestess looked like she was going to advance as well, but two more from Team 2 stepped in front of her, arms crossed, shaking their heads.

Church watched this happen, smiled, and turned back to Countess.

"Keep your fancy Intel ideas to yourself," he said. "We have a plan, and we've been building it for over a year. You're not coming in here at the last minute and changing anything."

Countess smoldered. Her hand twitched toward her dagger, but discipline caught the impulse mid-wrist.

Church felt the movement and trapped her hand. In a blur, a machete cleared leather—edge kissing her throat without a tremor.

The weapon was beautiful and lethal—clearly custom-made. The handle was smooth dark wood, and the blade bore an intricate swirl pattern.

"Best thing you can do is stay out of our way. If we say move, you move. If we say shoot, you shoot. No questions. Understood?"

Church didn't wait for her to respond.

"You're dismissed," he said. Then walked away. The rest of his team fell in behind him after shooting hostile looks at Countess's team.

* * *

Countess found Holly near the briefing stage, hologram projectors still flickering behind her like dying stars.

"Holly," she said quietly, approaching.

The petite doll turned, smile intact. "Yes, Countess?"

"I'm not sure what I'm doing here… what my team is doing here."

"How so?" asked Holly.

"We're being added to a large force that has been planning for over a year. We're a liability at best."

"I don't see it that way," said Holly. "Do your best and follow the orders of those appointed over you. It is nothing you haven't done a thousand times."

"Yes, but—"

Holly shot Countess a serious look. Her eyes glowed blue for a moment, then faded.

Countess abandoned the subject, then continued.

"We need better access to the full-immersion training rooms," she said. "The simulators aren't enough. Not for what you're asking."

"I'm sorry," Holly said, shaking her head, the motion almost human. "Priority access is allocated to Teams 1 and 2."

Countess clenched her fists. "So we're supposed to train for a suicide mission using half-broken VR pods while the golden boys get the good stuff?"

"You have simulators," Holly said gently. "Use them wisely."

"And the plan—" Countess pressed. "It's a blunt instrument. No finesse. Are you sure this is the best way?"

Holly's smile didn't waver. But her voice sharpened, just slightly.

"Just do as you're told," she said. "And do your best to survive."

Countess stood there for a moment, feeling the conversation slam shut like a vault door. The smile didn't fade, but something cold moved behind her eyes—a depth Countess had never seen before.

"Understood," she said finally, voice low.

As she turned away, she caught Stitch and Lin waiting at the edge of the room, both watching her carefully.

Outside, the walls of Highpoint Connector seemed to press closer, the steel skeleton of a world that had already started to collapse.

* * *

The briefing dispersed in a low thrum of boots, murmurs, and thinly masked tension.

Countess stood a moment longer, watching the flow of bodies, the quick alliances forming and re-forming in the corners of the theater.

Priestess, Lin, and Stitch approached her cautiously.

"Orders?" Lin asked, always blunt.

"You're dismissed for the day," Countess said. "Go get some rest. We'll regroup tomorrow."

Lin gave a short nod. Stitch hesitated like he might say something—then thought better of it and followed Lin toward the exit. Priestess raised her eyebrows meaningfully, then walked away as if she had serious thoughts on what had just transpired.

Countess exhaled slowly, the kind of breath you took when you knew there was no one left to see you break.

She crossed the wide floor to the bank of elevators near the far wall.

Only one stood open—a glass-back model designed for VIPs, no doubt, but tonight it was empty and waiting. She stepped inside and tapped the dining/recreation level.

The doors whispered shut behind her.

The car began its slow descent, and the landscape of the Highpoint Connector unrolled before her: a cavernous warehouse stretching down into the shadows, alive with movement.

Hundreds of logistics robots zipped along programmed routes, hauling crates, weapons, equipment—all the raw materials for a war none of them fully understood. They moved with perfect efficiency. No hesitation. No fear. No mistakes.

Not like us, Countess thought bitterly.

The elevator drifted lower, past rows of automated assembly lines, power stations blinking with indifferent light. In every direction, the pulse of a machine world preparing for slaughter.

Her team—the tenth and final—had been given the scraps. Broken simulators. Hand-me-down gear. No place at the table. And in thirteen days, they'd be thrown against the most lethal fortress left on the planet.

Countess leaned one shoulder against the glass, feeling the vibration of the gears as they descended.

It was hopeless.

It was rigged.

And yet, somewhere inside her rising despair, a small, sharp thought took root.

A counterweight. A way forward.

Her reflection stared back at her in the glass—pale, hollow-eyed, but still standing.

Still thinking. Still fighting.

Countess straightened as the elevator neared the bottom.

The robots below scurried, oblivious. The system trusted in its perfect design.

Good, she thought. Let them.

She smiled—a small, hard thing—as the doors slid open.

And she walked into the dim hallway.

6

Training had gone better than anyone expected. Even confined to the battered simulators, Team 10 was pulling together—slow at first, but steady. Stitch had stopped second-guessing the battle plans. Lin was hitting harder and moving faster.

Priestess, despite a rocky start adapting to Yorke Kingdom's more rigid style of warfare, was finding her footing. Countess gave her space. Growth took time—especially for someone who had never really been allowed to belong.

Tonight, the lounge on the recreation level was dark except for a few low wall lights and the ghostly shimmer of the cityscape holodisplay humming in the far corner. The door was closed—locked—for a quiet conspiracy.

The night after the briefing, Countess had been handed a mysterious note: her team was invited to a private meeting in the lounge, and told to inform no one.

Countess sat at the center of it all, flanked by Lin and Priestess, with Stitch fidgeting nearby, tapping his knee.

Across from them sat the ragtag clusters of Teams 7, 8, and 9—all latecomers. And, like Team 10, all were outcasts of the Strike Force. None were polished soldiers like those on Teams 1 and 2, but they were all survivors, and maybe that mattered more.

Will Ventor, leader of Team 9, was a compact, sharp-eyed man with a soldier's economy of motion. Natalie Fury lounged beside him, all casual muscle and barely contained energy, cleaning and disassembling a large machine gun. Arnold Blinker, their support specialist and medic, was disassembling and categorizing the contents of a large kit. He looked up and scanned the room occasionally through round, brass-rimmed glasses that didn't seem to belong to this century.

Team 8 was led by Will Harker, a warrior who defined the term cool. His hair was slicked back and he wore sunglasses all the time. Two pistols were mounted horizontally on the front of his chest rig for easy access. To his left and right were Dan Emmer and Amy Shay. Emmer was a big man, both tall and wide; even sitting, he towered over everyone in the room. Amy was the opposite. At five-five, she was the smallest person present.

Team 7 sprawled more loosely—Mark Tinkor with a

perpetual sly grin; Sarah Taylor perched quietly at the end of a couch, eyes bright and calculating; Jean Soldier (yes, that was his real name) and Greg Spye, both rough and practical sorts, were actually wrestling when Countess's team arrived.

Countess studied them all carefully. No one here wore the polish of the inner circle. No one here had been given priority gear or extra sim time. They were all the disposable ones.

Good. Those were the ones who had something real to fight for.

"We all know the official plan," Countess said finally, breaking the silence.

"Overwhelm them. Smash through the front doors. Rely on numbers and firepower."

She let the words hang a beat, heavy in the air.

"But we also know how that's gone in the past. Every attempt—failure."

Will Ventor nodded slowly. "So what are you suggesting?"

"A contingency," Countess said. "Something quiet. Parallel to the main strike."

Taylor leaned forward, voice low. "You're talking about

defying direct orders."

"No," Countess said smoothly. "I'm talking about surviving.

If—when—the main force gets bogged down, we break off.

We find another way inside. A workaround."

The room buzzed with quiet, nervous energy.

"And you have a plan?" Harker asked, pushing the sunglasses up the bridge of his nose.

Countess tilted her head toward Stitch.

Stitch cleared his throat awkwardly but met the room's gaze.

"I've been studying the schematics Holly gave us," he said. "And there are... gaps. Service tunnels. Emergency access routes. Old maintenance zones. They aren't on the main maps."

"Buried systems," Blinker muttered, rubbing his jaw. "Makes sense. No fortress survives on brute force alone. It survives on redundancy."

Stitch nodded, gaining steam.

"We can use TacCom to tap into the facility's feeds once they're fully active—map live data, track movements, find or make new vulnerabilities.

We won't hack the system head-on; security's too tight. But we might be able to slip in a side door."

"Subvert the network from inside," Spye added, smiling thinly. "I like it. Old-school guerrilla shit."

Taylor tapped a finger against her temple, thoughtful.

"Assuming we don't get shot by our own side."

"Better than getting crushed by the enemy," Lin said flatly.

"And don't forget what's running the show over there," Stitch added.

"Yeah," said Shay. "Some AI—control program. IDUB, I think it calls itself."

"I've heard its voice in the replays," Tinkor said. "It… mocks you while you're fighting. Creepy."

Countess waited, letting them feel the weight of it.

Finally, Will Ventor broke the silence.

"We're in."

"Us too," said Tinkor, grinning like he was about to pick a fight he actually liked.

Harker didn't respond right away. His face was inscrutable behind his sunglasses.

"Well," he said. "I don't like any of this, to be honest. But we'd better stick together, because I know this whole shit-show is gonna come off the rails. We're with you."

Countess nodded once.

"This isn't mutiny," she said, voice firm. "We fight with them—until it's clear we can't win their way."

"And then?" Fury asked.

"Then we fight smarter."

She leaned forward, looking each of them in the eye in turn.

"Like Stone said: live together. Die alone."

The others echoed the old phrase softly, like an oath.

Outside the locked lounge, the Highpoint Connector churned on, oblivious.

Inside, something new had taken root—quiet, desperate, defiant.

A real chance.

The first, fragile step toward saving themselves.

* * *

Team 9 filed out of the lounge with the others, all business on the surface. As the tide of Strike Force chatter flowed toward the lift shaft, Ventor gestured subtly and peeled his squad off into a quiet alcove—an old equipment room two levels down, long stripped of anything useful.

They didn't speak until the doors sealed behind them.

Ventor cracked his neck and turned to face them. "Well," he said. "Thoughts?"

Natalie Fury leaned against a deactivated console, arms crossed. "It's a bold move. She thinks she can pull this off?"

Blinker snorted. "Yeah. 'Unite the teams. Synchronize objectives. Seize the day.' Does she sound like Holly's star pupil to anyone else?"

"She's not," Ventor said. "She's improvising."

"So were the last three who tried to 'unify' the Force," Fury muttered. "You remember what happened to them?"

"I do," Ventor said. "I also remember they weren't half as organized as she is. And none of them walked out of Aether Storm. Countess did."

That quieted the room.

Blinker chewed his lip. "Still. We don't know her. We don't know what game she's playing."

"No," Ventor agreed. "But we know the one Teams 1 and 2 are playing. And that game is suicide."

He stepped into the center of the room, meeting each of their eyes.

"She made her case. It wasn't dumb. She's looking for a coordinated push, not a power grab. That's rare."

"So what's the play?" Fury asked.

"We hedge," Ventor said. "We show face with Teams 1 and 2 for now—stick to the op as briefed. But if things go sideways—and I think they will—we break to her side."

"You think she can actually lead?" Blinker asked.

"I think she already is," Ventor said. "Before tonight, no one wanted to step up. But she did—right away. That's important. Seems to come naturally to her."

"We'll see," said Fury. She looked concerned.

Another silence followed. Not uncertain—just thoughtful.

Finally, Fury nodded. "Okay. I'm in."

Blinker sighed, then shrugged. "Yeah. Backup plans never hurt."

Ventor gave a tight, satisfied nod.

"Countess may not be our friend," he said. "But if this

goes the way I think it will… she might be the only one who can get us out of Iroquois Warpath alive."

7

The train stretched like a steel snake through the loading bay, its dark-gray cars gleaming under the high arc lights of Highpoint Connector. Countess stood on the platform's edge, helmet clipped to her belt, arms folded, watching the flood of activity.

Machine guns. Rocket launchers. Heavy drones with twin-mounted autocannons. Missile pods. Smart mines.

Pallets of ammo stacked taller than a person.

Combat suits, portable barricades, demolition charges—the lifeblood of war, packed into crates marked with hazard warnings and priority seals.

The entire Strike Force moved with grim efficiency, loading gear into the logistics cars under Holly's careful supervision.

Her childlike holographic form walked up and down the line, calling out corrections, offering polite course adjustments, praising units that moved fastest.

"You're doing great," Holly said at one point, her voice warm and sweet enough to make Countess's skin crawl.

Off to the side, Natalie Fury from Team 9 ran a belt through a squat machine gun, slapping the top cover and timing her reload to a silent metronome in her HUD.

Blinker, their medic, popped auto-injectors from a foam tray and pressure-checked tourniquets on a volunteer's arm—counting capillary refill, nodding once, repacking with surgical neatness.

Sarah Taylor flicked a microdrone from her palm; the needle-sized camera stitched a quick LIDAR of the bay before perching back on her wrist like a steel moth.

Amy Shay hunched over a fried scout optic, soldering a new ribbon cable in place, the tiny plume of flux smoke curling blue in the arc lights.

Harker stood at a cold-range board, practicing cross-draw double taps with empty pistols—click–click, reholster, repeat—his form machine-clean.

Emmer and Jean Soldier traded slow, heavy sparring in exo-gloves, the pads thudding like distant drums.

Greg Spye chalked breach angles on a crate lid, laying out demo charges in a neat fan as if arranging organs for transplant.

Near one of the freight cars, Stitch struggled to wedge an oversized crate of drone chassis onto a pallet jack. Lin moved to help, the two of them muttering under their breath.

Priestess stood nearby, quietly cataloging their team's assigned equipment in her HUD.

Everything seemed smooth.

But Countess felt it—the hairline cracks beneath the surface.

Tense shoulders. Snapped words between squads. Operatives checking and rechecking their weapons with frantic fingers.

And when one of the loader bots stuttered—jerking sideways with a screech of metal before correcting itself—a low, collective murmur rolled across the bay.

Nobody said anything. But everyone heard it.

Even the machines seemed nervous.

* * *

Lin grunted as he staggered up the loading ramp, balancing an oversized crate against his shoulder.

The thing looked heavy enough to crush a normal man flat.

Countess caught sight of the crate's label as he

passed.

Stenciled in blocky, industrial letters:

OFFENSIVE DRONE, VTOL, HIGH-EXPLOSIVE

She stopped him with a sharp look.

"What the hell is that?"

"Just a little insurance," Lin said, setting the crate down with a heavy thud that rattled the ramp. "You know. For emergencies."

Countess scanned the rest of the gear already piled into the train—disciplined, precise, necessary. It was overkill in her opinion.

"Leave it," she said, already turning away. "We're not going to need anything like that."

Lin watched her walk off, her back straight, her voice already barking new orders at the next team. He smiled to himself, and loaded the crate anyway.

* * *

The train was finally loaded.

It had taken hours longer than expected. Tempers frayed. Backs ached. And now, standing on the platform in the waning light, most of the Strike Force looked like they'd already marched halfway through a war zone.

Final checks were complete. Weapons stowed. Gear

tagged and locked. A few last-minute crates of munitions and rations had been hauled aboard by groaning loaders. Every team had run their lists twice—some, three times.

Then a message appeared on their heads-up displays.

[TACCOM]: NOTICE—MANDATORY ASSEMBLY. GATHER ON PLATFORM.

They assembled in knots and clusters, weary and unspeaking.

Holly was waiting for them.

She stood atop an empty wooden crate—the tallest object nearby. Her arms were folded behind her back, head tilted slightly in that perfectly rehearsed gesture of optimism. The overhead work lights haloed her black holographic hair with a soft, flickering glow.

Countess spotted several squad leaders exchanging looks. Priestess leaned against a railing, arms crossed. Lin stood motionless at her side, face unreadable.

Holly beamed.

"I was planning to deliver the final briefing now," she said, chipper as ever. "But wow. That took more effort than even I expected!"

She scanned the crowd. Her voice didn't quite match the weight in their faces—the dust-streaked exhaustion, the thousand-yard stares.

She softened her tone.

"I can see you're tired. And I want you at your best for the real mission."

A pause, almost theatrical.

"So—change of plans."

She lifted her chin a little higher.

"We'll hold the final briefing first thing tomorrow. You've earned the rest. Tonight is yours. Sleep well. Dream better."

That last line landed… strangely.

A few team members turned and looked at each other. One of the engineers on Team 6 raised his eyebrows. Someone in the back murmured, "Dream better?"

No one laughed.

Holly just kept smiling—bright, unwavering, too still for comfort.

Then her avatar blinked out.

There was a long moment of silence.

Countess frowned. Just slightly. She'd heard a lot of

things from Holly. But that one felt... wrong.

The crowd began to disperse.

Countess lingered, watching the empty crate. The wood creaked in the settling air.

Then she turned and followed the others toward the barracks.

8

The barracks were quiet. The hum of the rail system echoed faintly through the floor, a distant heartbeat beneath the steel bones of Highpoint Connector. Countess sat alone at the edge of her bunk, boots off, gloves tucked beneath her belt. A datapad glowed dimly in her lap, illuminating her face with cold light.

She wasn't sleeping tonight. She already knew it.

She'd been trying not to think about Vorpal Vale.

The orphanage had been gray and cold, but never cruel. Her earliest memories were of concrete courtyards, chalk circles, and whispered promises passed between children who didn't know what futures they were being shaped for.

When the recruiters came, they didn't smile. They scanned, they sorted, they selected. Countess had passed every test with quiet precision. Too quiet, maybe. The others never spoke to her after that.

She had been ten.

The datapad buzzed softly as the playback resumed.

TacCom footage. No audio.

It showed a Strike Force—designation and timestamp redacted—caught in a hostile corridor inside some structure she didn't recognize. The video had been cropped, zoomed. It showed just enough.

Figures in full combat gear. Suppression fire. Then—

Chaos.

The kill zone bloomed in an instant. Flashes of plasma. Crumpled armor. A mech's frame igniting from the inside. One operative tried to crawl toward cover, dragging half a body.

Countess didn't blink, but her jaw clenched.

She paused the video.

The screen froze on a single frame—three operatives down, their Core-Tex units exposed and flickering, just visible beneath shattered skulls and ruptured gear.

She zoomed in.

The Core-Tex: a glossy, semi-clear hemisphere showing the brain underneath. It pulsed faintly. Still active.

Do they feel it?

Do they know?

She imagined them left there—still alive, in a way. Waiting. Whispering into the void.

Or maybe someone came and recovered them. Recycled them. Plugged them into new Operarius bodies. Memories wiped. New names. New jobs. New wars.

Do they remember who they were before? Too many questions, and none that Holly would ever answer.

She shut off the pad.

In the dark, Countess leaned back against the wall and closed her eyes.

The day had been long. Tomorrow would be worse.

The thought she wouldn't admit aloud—not to Lin, not even to Priestess—was the smallest and sharpest of all:

What happens if I fail?

Would she be remembered? Or would Holly frown, log the data, and move on?

Recompile the asset. Upload to the next viable host.

The words didn't exist anywhere official. But in the dead of night, she could almost hear them.

* * *

The cargo bay was dark and mostly empty—just a few supply crates stacked near the walls and an old forklift in standby mode. A faint orange light pulsed above the door, casting long, slow-moving shadows across the deck.

Lin sat cross-legged in the center of the room, hands resting lightly on his knees. Eyes closed. Breathing controlled. The only sound was the distant mechanical churn of the rail system vibrating through the walls.

He hadn't spoken to anyone since Holly dismissed the crowd. He didn't need to.

He let his breath settle.

The pain always came second—that's what they taught him. In the Corps, pain wasn't a warning; it was punctuation. It meant you'd already made a mistake. The first time he'd broken a rib, he'd cried out. The second time, he hadn't.

By the fifth, he didn't even flinch.

They taught him silence. Stillness. And how to react to

his injuries only after the enemy had stopped moving.

Eventually, he'd stopped thinking of himself as a man. He was something narrower. Sharper.

A tool doesn't ask questions. It gets the job done— simply and efficiently.

He became the blade they sent into places no one else came back from.

Over time, he noticed a shift in his instructors. His peers. Something in their eyes. Not pride. Not awe.

Fear.

Lin opened his eyes. The bay remained unchanged. Still and humming.

A single light blinked over the doorframe, counting time. Not for them—for the train. For the battle to come.

He let his mind drift to a memory—one that returned more often lately.

His final instructor. An older man with one leg and a voice like cracking ice. After the last trial, he pulled Lin aside—not to congratulate him, but to mark him.

"We're not here to survive," the man said. "We're here to ensure that Yorke Kingdom endures. It's a legacy for all of us. For our children... and our children's children."

That was the moment Lin understood: he wasn't just killing for command. He was preserving a thread. One that had to stretch across centuries, no matter how many people it cut along the way.

He exhaled slowly and closed his eyes again.

They would be arriving at Iroquois Warpath soon. He wasn't afraid.

But he wondered—just a little—what would remain if they failed.

And if he fell... would anyone even remember the blade?

* * *

The dormitory lights were dimmed to rest-cycle mode. Pale blue washed across the bulkhead. Vents hissed quietly overhead.

Priestess sat cross-legged on her bunk, spine straight, hands folded in her lap.

She wasn't asleep. She wasn't meditating.

She was trying to pray.

But it wasn't the same—not here. Not in this cold place of alloy and angles. No flame. No stone. No pulse of warmth beneath her feet. No soft echo from the cave walls.

Just her. A woman too far from Amenigoth. Too far from Sky Mother.

Back home, the Cave had been alive. Breathing. A womb of earth and fire, its walls slick with minerals that shimmered like constellations. That's where she'd heard the voice for the first time.

I need your help, Sky Mother had said. Not a voice, exactly. Not sound.

But knowing—inside her mind.

Here, there was only silence.

She whispered words out of habit, but they landed dead on the air. No spark. No charge. Nothing sacred.

She opened her eyes.

She tried to distract herself—pulled up a poetry file, one of the old verses from her schooling, the kind meant to anchor her spirit in times of doubt. She scrolled a few lines, then stopped.

It felt hollow.

Even the words had lost their weight out here.

She closed the file.

Her HUD flickered briefly, waiting for input.

She hesitated, then pulled up the internal security feeds.

One by one, the views appeared—grainy monochrome angles of the Connector's interior. Storage bays. Hallways. The barracks. The train platform.

She saw Stitch laughing at something Lin said. She saw Team 9 breaking down and repacking their gear, double-checking inventory they'd already checked an hour ago. She saw Countess alone in her bunk, unmoving, her datapad's glow the only motion in the frame.

She muted the audio. Just watched.

For a long time.

They all seemed so fragile—the way she felt.

How many of them would die tomorrow?

She didn't ask Sky Mother.

She already knew the answer.

* * *

Stitch sat cross-legged on his bunk, a ration bar in one hand and a comm slate in the other. The bar was untouched. The slate blinked at him, cursor waiting like it expected a confession.

He exhaled through his nose and muttered, "Let's try this again."

He started typing.

To whoever finds this: Hey. I was the funny one. The smartass. The guy with the bad jokes and better hacks. And if you're reading this, it means I probably—

He stopped.

Deleted it.

"Too dramatic," he whispered.

He tried again.

Countess, Lin, Priestess—

If I don't make it, I just want you to know I—

Deleted.

Hey, so. Tomorrow's the big day. Just wanted to—

Deleted.

He tossed the slate onto the mattress and lay back with a groan, one arm flung across his face.

The silence was unbearable. Not like his old Yorke barracks, where everything buzzed and blinked and pulsed with life. Highpoint was too quiet. Too still. Like the world was holding its breath, waiting to break.

He sat up again. Swore under his breath.

Stared at the slate.

Then, finally, started typing without editing himself:

COUNTESS—

I know I messed up. I was trying to impress you. Thought maybe you'd see something in me besides the loudmouth. Thought maybe I could be more.

LIN—

You don't have to like me. But you fight like hell in that sim. I see it. I'm gonna do better. You'll see.

PRIESTESS—

Still not sure if you're going to stab me or save me. But I respect you either way. You've got more weight in your stare than most people have in their whole squad.

If tomorrow's a mess… I'll be there.

No more solo plays.

—Stitch

He sat back. Read it twice.

Didn't delete it.

Didn't send it, either.

He saved it to the slate's private log, encrypted it under a laughably weak passcode: IAMREADY.

Then he turned off the lights, lay back on his bunk, and stared at the ceiling until the shapes stopped moving.

9

The Briefing Theater felt different this time. The air was heavier, charged with a low, eager energy. Weapons were stowed, gear bags tucked neatly at the sides of boots. There was no more training. No more simulations.

This was it.

Rows of armored soldiers filled the tiered benches—all in combat gear, faces dimly lit by the massive display wall ahead. The hum of the ventilation system and a low murmur of whispered anticipation were the only sounds.

Then—without warning—the lights dimmed.

All of the voices fell silent.

The room lights flared bright momentarily, revealing Holly—not as a hologram this time, but standing in the flesh. Her childlike frame, immaculate uniform, and polished black boots made her look eerily out of place among the armored giants around her.

When she spoke, her tone was warm, smooth, and rehearsed to the syllable.

"Good morning, Strike Force. I see morale is high."

Nervous chuckles. A few murmured "ma'am"s from the front rows.

"I wanted to be here in person," Holly continued, her gaze sweeping the room, "because what we begin today will decide whether this world lives or dies. You all know the mission's promise—inside Iroquois Warpath lies technology capable of restoring our environment, our food, even our air. But the facility is still defended by an autonomous system that has repelled every attempt to breach it for centuries. That ends now."

Her tone hardened, and she folded her hands neatly behind her back.

"You have one objective: crack the fortress and secure the recovery technology. Commanders Stone and Church will brief you on the details of the operation."

Holly stepped back, then turned and disappeared into the shadows.

A deep, resonant blast shook the room.

It wasn't music. It was a horn—ancient, thunderous, vibrating through the steel floor. The kind of sound that carried across centuries of war. Dust shivered from the rafters. The front rows looked like their hair was caught in a silent wind.

And then a voice boomed through the speakers:

"STONE AND CHURCH PRESENT…"

The phrase hung in the air like the opening crawl of some over-the-top war film.

A ripple of laughter erupted from the front benches— Team 4, of course. They couldn't help it.

Church's mic cut with a hiss as he vaulted forward, machetes already half drawn.

"You…!" He pointed one gleaming blade straight at Team 4. "Shut up!"

That only made them laugh harder.

"The Raid on Iroquois Warpath," said Church's voice again, louder this time and forced into theatrical gravitas.

Now the whole room was snickering.

Stone stood beside him, arms crossed, shaking his head. "I told you," he said quietly.

Church glared at him, then at the laughing operatives.

Finally, with a sharp motion, he slammed both machetes back into their sheaths.

"God… damn it!"

He stormed offstage, muttering something that made Stone sigh like a man who'd seen this movie before.

The laughter slowly died, leaving behind a charged, uneasy silence.

"All right," Stone said. "Let's try this again—minus the theatrics."

He stepped forward, the holo-model of Iroquois Warpath slowly spinning behind him. The hologram angled down so the view looked down into the top of the facility. It locked to a close-up of the outer ring. The cavernous schematic glowed with layers—perimeter fields, sentry corridors, power arteries—each labeled in crisp type.

"This is where the battle will take place. The outer security perimeter: Red Sector A."

He pulled the short sword from its sheath on his lower back.

"The Strike Force will enter here. These double doors will open for us, care of IDUB, the facility's security A.I. It always does this, as if daring the attacking force. We will stage our assault from inside."

Stone took a moment to scan the faces in the

audience.

"The plan is simple: three steps.

One: We gain access to the spawning area on the inner wall—here. Inside these doors, drones, robots, and other warforms are released onto the battlefield. The Vanguard Force, Team 2, led by Captain Church, will breach this area. Team 1, led by me, will provide close support. All others will provide cover and support to this effort.

Two: We have an opportunity to succeed here, courtesy of the previous Strike Force. Their video footage has revealed a critical vulnerability, previously unknown."

A grainy black-and-white video played in front of the hologram. It showed a team entering the doors to the Spawning Area. At the center of the room was a tall column covered in blinking lights and video displays.

"Careful analysis of this structure, which we're calling the Control Tower, shows that it likely controls the release of the drone and robot dispensers. As you can see, the lights seem to correspond to release of these drones—here, here, and here."

The footage ran for a few seconds longer, then abruptly cut off.

"So our second objective is to destroy this Control Tower."

Stone cleared his throat.

"Three: Breach the inner wall of the Spawning Area. This octagonal center section is Iroquois Warpath. Once the Control Tower is taken out, we set off explosive charges on the inner wall here, then enter to gain access to the facility proper. With luck, we'll secure Iroquois Warpath in fifteen minutes.

To review:

Step 1: Access the Spawning Area.

Step 2: Destroy the Control Tower.

Step 3: Breach Inner Wall."

The hologram dimmed back to its idle spin as a low murmur—some skeptical, some anxious—rippled through the theater.

"That's all I have. I'll let Captain Church wrap this up."

Church reappeared, looking much more composed than when he'd left. He walked to center stage and addressed the assembly in a strong, confident voice.

"TacCom will provide battlefield command and control. It's the most powerful tool in our arsenal, but it can be jammed or spoofed—so be on guard."

He took a deep breath, then continued.

"Timing is everything. TacCom will provide synchronized windows for us to operate in. Our estimate: from entry to breach of the Spawning Area is five minutes. Destruction of the Control Tower, another five—

give or take thirty seconds. Video archives indicate the opposing force achieves overwhelming strength at the fifteen-minute mark. So we get thirteen minutes to complete our objectives. Make them count."

Church turned and walked to the side of the stage. Stone took his place.

"If there are no questions…"

Countess stood. "I have a question, sir."

Church frowned and shook his head.

Commander Stone blinked and sighed. "Go ahead, Countess."

"Respectfully," Countess continued, "what happens when we get inside? Do the security forces just… stop fighting?"

Stone raised his eyebrows. "Well—"

"I'll answer that," said Holly, emerging once more from the shadows. "And it's a valid question."

Holly directed her focus at Countess. "I've studied all of the insecure communications to and from the facility—everything that isn't encrypted. Several conversations suggest that security units, and combat in general, are not permitted within the facility."

Priestess stood up beside Countess. "Suggest?"

"Strongly imply," Holly corrected lightly.

"And that's good enough for me," said Stone, putting the matter to rest.

"And as a reminder"—Stone gave Countess an exasperated look—"the destruction of the Control Tower will likely stop the flow of additional units onto the battlefield."

He scanned the audience one last time. "Okay, let's wrap this up. We launch in two hours, so make your final preparations. Sleep if you can. Eat if you must. Dismissed."

The theater emptied in a hush. Countess stayed seated a moment longer, watching the hologram of Iroquois Warpath spin slowly in the empty air. She stood, heart steadying like a drum in the dark, and joined her team.

10

The teams filed onto the passenger cars once the cargo was secured. Countess found a seat along the wall of Car 7, her team clustering nearby, while Teams 8 and 9 settled across the aisle. The air smelled of oil, sweat, and ozone—the scent of a building storm.

Down the narrow corridor, she caught sight of Commander Stone standing at the head of Car 1. He was speaking with Church and a few other inner-circle officers—laughing, relaxed.

They're already celebrating, she thought grimly.

Countess turned her gaze back to her own people.

Lin dozed lightly, arms folded, feigning indifference.

Priestess sat rigidly upright, eyes half-lidded but alert.

Stitch fidgeted, tapping a rapid, anxious rhythm against his rifle stock.

The doors slid closed. The train lurched forward with a mechanical shudder, and the platform lights fell away behind them.

Around them, the soldiers of the Strike Force fell into small rituals—fragments of training and nerves.

One man stripped and reassembled his rifle over and over, the metallic clicks sharp in the stale air.

Two medics compared bandage loads in silence, neither meeting the other's eyes.

Someone down the car was already asleep, mouth open, snoring softly beneath the hum of the rails.

Another soldier—young, broad-shouldered, terrified— stood up and shouted, "We're gonna tear that place apart! Nothing's gonna stop us!" His voice cracked halfway through, but nobody corrected him. A few answered with tired cheers. Then the quiet, low-level tension returned.

Through the narrow windows, the train tunneled ever deeper underground—the reinforced walls slick with age and condensation, concrete girders flashing past like the ribs of a dying giant.

There were no stars here. No open sky.

Only miles of cold, black earth pressing down.

Gradually, the track leveled out.

The vibrations shifted—heavier now, more hollow—as they entered the outer perimeter of Iroquois Warpath.

The lighting changed too: from the warm orange sodium lamps of Highpoint to harsh bluish fluorescents, each one buzzing and flickering as if struggling to stay alive.

And then, outside the windows—the arrival platform.

A vast, cavernous expanse of pitted concrete, half-devoured by rust and mold. Towering gantries leaned overhead like skeletal fingers. Abandoned service vehicles sat frozen in thick layers of dust, their tires rotted into the floor.

It was a forgotten graveyard—a descent into a place that had already buried everyone who came before.

As the train thundered toward it, a voice came over the internal speakers—Holly, as always, chipper and bright.

"Attention, Strike Force.

Final staging in thirty minutes.

Please ensure all personal and team equipment are accounted for.

Remember: victory favors the prepared."

The message echoed briefly through the cars before cutting off, leaving only the low rumble of the rails and the metallic pulse of inevitability.

Countess closed her eyes briefly, feeling the steady

vibration under her boots.

Soon, it would all come apart. She knew it.

But not yet.

She opened her eyes, meeting Lin's across the aisle. He nodded once—a silent agreement.

They were ready. Whatever that meant now.

The train surged onward, slowing now—a black arrow aimed straight at hell.

* * *

The air in the outer perimeter was cold, metallic, and stale—the smell of too many years spent sealed beneath the earth.

Floodlights bathed the staging zone in a harsh, sterile glow, throwing long, warped shadows across the pitted concrete. It was as unfinished and unwelcoming as a tomb.

The train cars hissed and groaned as the teams unloaded their gear.

The mood had changed.

The same men and women who had joked and shouted on the ride down now moved in near-silence, eyes down, hands busy.

One soldier muttered the words to a prayer under his breath as he checked the safety on his rifle for the fifth time.

Another stared blankly at the enormous doors ahead, his jaw working soundlessly.

The loud one—the same young soldier who'd boasted, "We're gonna tear that place apart"—was quiet now. He stood frozen beside his pack, watching frost collect on the floor beneath the floodlights. His lips moved once, shaping words no one could hear.

Even the medics had stopped talking, their movements clipped and precise. Every sound—the rattle of ammo belts, the clank of boots, the rasp of fabric—felt magnified in the vacuum of fear.

Countess moved among the chaos, silent and sharp-eyed, absorbing everything—the nervous way Stitch kept tugging at his gloves, the quiet precision with which Lin double-checked every latch and strap, the way Priestess slipped through the sea of crates and bodies like a blade, eyes scanning, shoulders loose but ready.

And looming ahead, waiting for them all, were the enormous red double doors stenciled in heavy black letters:

SECURITY – SECTOR A

Each door was three stories high, reinforced steel layered with some kind of unknown composite, worn smooth by the passage of centuries.

Beyond them waited the enemy.

And beyond the enemy—the objective. The treasure they came for, hidden somewhere inside.

Countess knelt near a pallet stacked with missile cases, sketching rough mental maps of what lay beyond the doors to Sector A. She didn't like it.

Near the front of the crowd, a makeshift platform had been rigged out of a cargo hauler bed. Stone climbed onto it, Church following a step behind, grinning like a wolf at a feast. The murmurs died.

Countess rose and drifted toward her team, standing shoulder to shoulder with Lin, Priestess, and Stitch as the Strike Force assembled.

Stone's voice rang out, crisp and commanding:

"Today," he said, "we finish what others could not.

The world above is dying—and we are here to find the tools to heal it."

He gestured grandly to the towering Sector A doors behind him.

"The answers lie here—buried beneath the lies of a

dead civilization.

We are the broadsword to cut through the dark.

We are the fire to burn away the rot."

Somewhere in the crowd, a voice whooped. Others joined, a rough chorus swelling up.

Stitch leaned close to Countess, whispering, "Sounds like he's already writing the history books."

Countess allowed herself a tiny, dry smile.

Good. Let them believe it.

Hope was a useful thing. Right up until the moment it broke.

Stone was suddenly interrupted by a loud screech from a white plastic speaker mounted above the security doors. Static hissed, faded, and then a voice came through—smooth, resonant, touched with amusement and disdain.

"Welcome, Strike Force operatives. I admire your conviction; it will be recorded."

The crowd stiffened. Weapons shifted in hands.

"However, please be advised: your arrival is unauthorized and your actions are classified as hostile. Your deaths, should you choose to proceed, will be your own responsibility."

A pause.

"If you wish to avoid the inevitable, I recommend an immediate and unconditional retreat. Otherwise... enjoy your final moments of free will."

The speaker emitted a grating squeal, then fell silent.

Silence gripped the staging area like a fist.

Nobody moved.

Then Church laughed—a big, barking thing meant to be infectious. Others joined, but their voices sounded strained, brittle.

Countess didn't laugh. She exchanged a glance with Priestess, who raised an eyebrow as if to say: Well. That just happened.

IDUB had spoken. Its intentions were clear. This was the point of no return.

Stone straightened on the platform, rallying the shaken crowd.

"Let it talk," he snarled. "Let it try to stand against us. IDUB will fall—just like everything else that stood against us."

Another cheer followed—louder, but thinner now, stretched tight with desperation.

Countess tightened the straps on her gauntlets, eyes locked on the massive doors. There were only two kinds of people beyond them: survivors and statistics.

The last quiet moment slipped away. Beyond those gates waited madness, slaughter, and the uncertain price of survival.

Act II
Iroquois Warpath

11

The doors groaned open with a sound like a dying leviathan—metal straining against rust and age. As the last bolt disengaged, the Strike Force surged forward, weapons raised, eyes scanning.

And then... they saw it.

The security perimeter stretched before them like the gaping maw of some long-starved beast—illuminated only by narrow strips of pale lights embedded in the ceiling.

It was a graveyard of forgotten battles.

A vast, aircraft hangar-sized chamber unfolded—wider than a football stadium, and so deep that the walls seemed to vanish into a gray haze. The ceiling disappeared into darkness. Broken gantries, high above, jutted at crooked angles like snapped ribs. The far end of the room was partially cloaked in shadow, and the inner wall of the facility was stenciled with large, red capital letters: SECURITY – SECTOR A.

No one spoke.

The air hit them like a wall—hot, damp and thick.

The scent of chemical rot punched through every filter in their helmets: scorched flesh, charred plastic, oxidized blood, ammonia and rust. Beneath it all was something older. Something human. Death was layered on older decomposition, all baked into the concrete over centuries of failed incursions.

Someone gagged.

Countess clenched her jaw, tasting the atmosphere like a poison wine. Iron. Sulfur. Powder residue. Char. The particulates clung to her tongue. Her eyes watered.

The floor beneath their boots was slick with old oil and dark, caked residue. Burn marks spiderwebbed across the ground. Shrapnel was fused into the concrete where explosions had atomized men and machines alike.

She stepped over a charred boot—still occupied.

Farther in, skeletal remains slumped against the bulkheads. Some still wore armor—half-melted or shattered. The faded logo of Phoenix was etched into their ruined chestplates, like an emblem for a failed ideology.

The lighting was thin and inadequate—narrow strips of flickering amber embedded in the walls, casting the space in a sickly gloom. Every movement threw monstrous shadows along cracked surfaces. At random intervals, the structure emitted deep groans, echoing through the chamber like whale-song from a nightmare.

"Eyes up," Stone barked over TacCom, but even his voice was tight.

The HUD overlays jittered. Signals pinged off inert debris, trying to make sense of a place long past reason.

Lin moved like a ghost, scanning every corner with sharp, controlled arcs. Priestess paused near a splatter of scorched blood that stretched across an entire support pillar, staring at it like a hieroglyph.

Stitch stepped carefully around a cluster of long-dead drones, their metal husks warped by heat. One had clawed thick, vertical grooves into the wall. Its faint red optical sensor stared—like the eye of a fallen soldier.

"This isn't a battlefield," he muttered. "It's a butcher shop."

"It's a cemetery," said Priestess, "with all the bodies exhumed and left out to decompose."

A silence followed, punctuated by a slow, distant creak—like something massive shifting its weight overhead.

Countess knelt, touching the floor. Her fingers came back black and gritty. The air felt heavier here, like it resisted their movement.

"So many…" she whispered.

The vanguard of the Strike Force moved through in tight formations, boots and treads grinding over the pitted floor. Weapons locked, gear heavy on their backs, breath tight in their throats.

When everyone was in position, they paused and quietly took in the horror of their surroundings. No one in their right mind should be here.

Somewhere behind them, gears shrieked and the doors rumbled shut—grinding closed with a finality that suggested no intention of opening again.

They were inside now.

No turning back.

1 2

The column began to move. Logistics crews hauled supply and turret crates deeper into the chamber, following TacCom-assigned grid coordinates. Fire teams swept forward in staggered lines, boots crunching over debris-strewn ground. Twisted weapons, charred ammo belts, and piles of slagged armor were fused to the floor. Half-melted assault drones lay collapsed like dead animals—their chassis curled inward, blackened spines exposed to the stagnant air.

Someone stumbled on a helmet. It slid forward and struck the wall with a soft, hollow clink. Inside it, a skull—half-shattered—grinned up through the cracked visor.

A younger soldier from Team 5 gagged, doubling over. His rifle clattered to the ground.

"Shit," someone whispered.

Countess didn't turn to look. She saw it in the corner of her HUD—multiple vitals spiking. Heart rates rising. Breathing erratic. Stress indicators lighting up orange.

A woman near the back of the line pressed a hand over her mouth, eyes wide and shimmering. Not crying. Not yet. But her shoulders shook as she stared at a mural of charred handprints along the wall—dozens of them, etched into the soot like ancient cave art.

Stitch coughed. "The air here..." he rasped, then spat black phlegm onto the floor. "It tastes like burnt wires and grave dust."

Even with rebreathers engaged, the environment was overwhelming. There was no circulation—just a thick, oily atmosphere, more particulate than air.

Eyes watered. Noses ran. More soldiers began to cough or wipe at their faces. Some pulled back their helmets to rub burning eyes, only to regret it the moment the raw stench hit them full-force.

Countess heard someone retching behind her. Not vomiting. Not yet. But close.

"Keep moving," she snapped.

A soldier dropped to one knee near a collapsed drone turret. It was still partially powered, its optic blinking weakly.

As he reached for it, the turret spasmed—just once— and then died with a crackle of blue sparks.

He scrambled backward, breath hitching in panic.

Another wept openly—silent tears cutting clean lines

through the grime on her face.

The devastation grew worse the farther they advanced. What looked at first like collapsed barricades were, in fact, ripped-open personnel carriers—torn apart by something with impossible strength. One of the APCs had been twisted into a pretzel of steel and composite, the interior walls still splashed with dried blood turned black with age.

Finally, Stone mounted a broken bulkhead like a pulpit, his voice cracking over TacCom.

"Enough."

The Strike Force hesitated. Movement stilled.

Stone had overall command; Church ran the assault teams. Together they'd trained the Strike Force for brutal situations—but never anything like Warpath.

Stone looked over the crowd with a face like carved granite. His voice was steady but sharp.

"We knew what we were walking into. We knew this would be ugly. You've trained for this. You've seen death before. This—" he gestured at the carnage "—is just another kind of battlefield."

He let that sink in.

"Focus on the objectives. Focus on your team. The ghosts here don't need our pity."

From the opposite flank, Church's voice joined in—rougher, more guttural.

"This place wants to break you. Wants you crying and puking so you miss what's about to attack. Don't give it that satisfaction. Hold the line."

"Secure the gear," Stone said. "Stick to your TacCom grid placements. Support units, deploy turrets and prepare for casualties. Heavy teams, prep your assault positions."

Countess exhaled—shaky, but steady enough. The command net refocused. Orders pinged out. Units snapped back into motion.

The horror wasn't gone, but it was pushed back—contained by habit, by leadership, by sheer survival instinct.

She glanced back once, just for a heartbeat, at the wall of scorched handprints.

So many had died trying.

But they weren't here for a history lesson.

They were here to win.

* * *

A voice emerged from the facility's public address system. It was smooth, mocking, and almost... delighted.

"Welcome, honored guests. I am the voice of Phoenix facility 11194, also known as Iroquois Warpath. IW for short, but most call me... IDUB.

It has been a considerable time since anyone was foolish enough to try what you are attempting. But alas, here we are again!"

All across the Strike Force's HUDs, waveform graphs jumped as IDUB's voice filled the air.

"And Holly," IDUB continued, "so persistent. So predictably stubborn.

Thousands of attempts, hundreds of years, all culminating in this final, desperate farce.

Is this all you have for me? Your finest? Or are they simply more grist for the mill?

We'll find out soon enough."

Several soldiers shifted nervously. A few tightened their grips on their rifles.

Holly's face appeared on their HUDs, calm and precise—her voice a surgical strike against the seeping doubt.

"It's programmed to demoralize you. Ignore it. Stick to

the plan."

Stone, leading the assault wedge, raised his hand and signaled the push forward. His voice was a hard whipcrack over TacCom.

"Perimeter breach teams, move up! Take your initial positions! We're not here to listen to fairy tales!"

The Strike Force surged forward into Red Sector A, spreading into preassigned battle cells.

Heavy weapon units rolled in armored crates; auto-turrets unfolded like mechanical flowers; drones deployed—all precisely choreographed.

Church, stalking alongside Stone, activated TacCom's tactical overlay for everyone.

"Remember the plan," he said. "We hit the Spawning Area—cut off the snake's head. Breach, flood. We disable the Control Tower. Fast and hard."

He slammed the stock of his rifle into his armored shoulder—a sharp, brutal punctuation mark.

IDUB's voice returned, lightly amused.

"I see... straight to business, then. Very well!"

Deep thuds vibrated through the floor—distant

mechanisms coming online.

Two enormous concrete walls on either side of the Strike Force rose slowly and met the ceiling high above. Sector A was now isolated from the other perimeter sectors—B, C, and D.

"The battle arena and rules of engagement are now set.

The doors are sealed. There is no escape.

Your survival clock has begun. And to honor your bravery... I extend this charity: I will tell you what is coming, when it's coming. I will announce every wave. I hope it helps!"

The massive bulkhead doors behind and to either side of the Strike Force locked with a ka-chunk of finality.

Ahead, at the far end of Sector A, four segmented gates groaned as their locking mechanisms disengaged and opened.

IDUB's voice grew almost musical, savoring the words:

"Let us begin... First wave: Basic Infantry Drones.

Good luck. You're gonna need it."

Rifles snapped up. Safeties clicked off.

Someone whispered a prayer.

The Strike Force braced—breath caught—as the first wave came pouring through the gates.

* * *

Fury, from Team 9, stepped forward and pulled a thin blanket off the massive gun she carried. Stenciled on the side, in fresh and partially dripping white paint, was the name SLEDGEHAMMER.

At six-foot-two, she towered over most of the Strike Force—a wall of solid muscle. But the .50-caliber GAU-21 assault cannon she brandished somehow made her look four times as massive.

Will Blinker, Team 9's medic, saw the artillery and took two steps back.

"My God, Fury," he said. "You gonna start a war with that thing?"

"Nope." She spat on the ground. "I'm gonna end one."

The first wave broke against them like water on rock.

The Strike Force moved as one—fluid and brutal. Infantry drones crumpled under precise gunfire. Auto-turrets spat streams of death into the choked corridors. Church's heavy weapons teams established kill zones that ground the advancing machines into smoking heaps.

Then the voice came again—smooth, savoring every syllable.

"Wave Two," said IDUB, almost purring. "Advanced drones. Enjoy."

The second wave hit—tougher, faster—but the Strike Force held.

Fury sent several rapid-fire volleys into the oncoming swarm. Everything she hit was reduced to glittering fragments of metal and smoke.

A few injuries barked across the comms—minor. No fatalities. Spirits surged.

When the third wave fell, Stone made the call.

"Vanguard team—move! Door Two! Target is highlighted in TacCom. Go, go, go!"

Their HUDs updated:

[TACCOM]: VANGUARD TEAM: MOVE TO TARGET.

A five-man team peeled off—Stone's best. Fast, coordinated, lethal.

A hundred meters ahead of the main line, the ground-level deployment door loomed—set into the reinforced wall like a black void. If they could breach it—disrupt the enemy flow at the source—they could get the main force inside, defend from there, and blow the inner wall to the facility. Second, it would get them out of Sector A, the open area that IDUB controlled.

The vanguard tore across the cratered floor, a blur of speed and firepower.

They moved inside, led by Church, like they'd practiced a hundred times. They secured the room and began laying down overlapping fire on any emerging machines.

Stone's team took their positions and covered Church's team from outside the spawning area.

Church approached the hulking Control Tower in the center of the room and began attaching explosive charges to the blinking control panels.

"Charges ready," he said. "Everyone take cover."

Church's team hid behind steel columns and the hulls of IDUB's fallen drones.

"Stand by... bang bang BANG!" Church squeezed the detonator paddle, and the room filled with yellow light.

The explosion flung chunks of the Control Tower past

them in all directions. When the pressure wave had passed, Church peeked. Only the base of the tower remained—a smoking pile of rubble.

"Wooo hooo!" someone cheered.

"Yeah!" shouted another.

Church stood and pounded his fists once against his armored chest plate.

"That's what I'm talking about."

Church put his hands on his hips, proud of his work.

"Good job, team," said Stone. "Prepare to—"

A loud squeal erupted from Sector A's PA, followed by the horrible sound of mechanical laughter.

"There's a void under the tower," said Countess. "I can see something—"

The rubble sank through the floor.

Silence held for a breath.

Then came the laughter again.

A fresh tower unfolded from the dark like steel petals, rising to its full height.

"No!" shouted Church. "It can't be!"

IDUB laughed even harder.

Then the door to the chamber slammed shut, and nearby, the drone spawners reactivated.

Stone tried to salvage the situation. He ordered an engineer forward with an explosive pack; when everyone was clear, it blew—leaving only a dark scorch on the door.

"Church, we can't get to you," said Stone. "Looks like you're on your own in there."

Drones poured into the spawning chamber and opened fire. The numbers were overwhelming, and one by one, the vanguard started to fall.

Church's eyes were wide and he was sweating hard. His blood went cold; his mind splintered.

In a panic, he threw himself at one of the consoles on the new Control Tower, desperate to stop the onslaught of new enemies.

Several of Church's team closed in on him, doing what they could to protect him. They fell, and within seconds, Church was left alone.

"This... this wasn't supposed to happen!" he shouted, feverishly jabbing at the keyboard. It had no effect. "This is my moment! I built the plan—it was perfect—"

Church turned. And when he saw he was completely surrounded, he backed against the Control Tower.

"I won!" he said with equal parts fury and fear. "This is my legacy."

Hundreds of drones floated motionless around him.

"Now you have nothing," whispered IDUB through his headset.

Church stared in horror, then began to shake violently as blue arcs of electricity shot out of the Control Tower and burned his flesh. Seconds later, his charred and lifeless body crumpled to the floor.

[TACCOM]: CAPT. CHURCH — SIGNAL LOST.

The channel hissed for a second—then silence. No one spoke.

13

Outside the spawning chamber, the floor erupted. From hidden ports in the walls and ground, automated defenses snapped to life. Gun turrets unfolded like mechanical spiders. Mines detonated in precise, terrible bursts.

One of the vanguard—O'Connor, quick and sharp-eyed—caught the first blast, thrown sideways like a rag doll. Another—Juno, the fastest runner—crumpled without a sound as shrapnel tore through his armor.

Concrete barriers slammed up from the floor with a seismic roar, cutting the vanguard team off from the main Strike Force.

From scorched and scarred public address speakers overhead, IDUB's voice returned, syrupy with mock regret:

"Oh, you thought you could stop my machines? How quaint.

Destroying the tower? A little obvious, don't you think?"

Stone's face had lost all its color. He'd watched in disbelief as his partner's team died. And it happened with such alarming speed he was tempted to think TacCom was broken.

Church himself had fallen last, but not before a truly terrifying outburst. Stone didn't know what to make of it. He'd sounded out of his mind. What hell had happened in there?

The spawning chamber doors flew open, and a dark flood of machines poured out. They fanned out and began firing with every weapon they had.

A barrage ripped into someone nearby.

A warm spray of blood to the face snapped Stone back into the fight.

He shouted orders—*fall back, fall back*—but the moving barriers turned their retreat into a bloodbath.

His comms were overloaded with screams, and two more were down before anyone could even move.

* * *

Across the battlefield, the Strike Force reeled.

"Barrier protocols active," Holly snapped. "Trying to override—"

Massive concrete slabs slid and locked into new formations, slicing Sector A into brutal, claustrophobic kill corridors.

What had been an open battlefield was now a twisting and lethal maze.

"Sector geometry access confirmed," Holly's voice hissed in their ears. "IDUB's running the floor plan changes live. I don't have control, but I can see the changes just before they happen. I'll display them for you as best I can. Stay sharp!"

Soldiers scrambled to reorient their HUDs as her live overlays flickered into place.

Stone rallied the survivors, his voice a lifeline against the rising tide of panic.

"Regroup! Suppressing fire! Cover the vanguard if you can!"

The walls narrowed.

The drones adapted.

The Strike Force's mobility vanished, swallowed whole by the shifting terrain.

IDUB watched, and waited.

Somewhere overhead, another mechanism groaned to life.

The walls breathed. For a heartbeat, nothing moved. The facility itself was exhaling—ready for the next kill.

* * *

The Strike Force fought to regroup.

In the narrow, brutalized corridors that Sector A had become, Blinker heroically dragged wounded into rough cover. The dead he left where they fell. There was nothing he could do for them.

Fury laid down fields of suppressing fire. She lost count of how many machines she'd reduced to scrap, and she was on her third barrel change. Something had to give, Fury thought. She was tired and her arm muscles burned.

The air smelled different now—sharp, metallic, buzzing with something just beyond hearing.

Every breath came a little harder. Every glance over a shoulder, just a little sharper.

Something was changing.

Somewhere overhead, deep within the facility's unseen guts, a low mechanical whine began to rise—not sudden, but gradual—like a storm gathering far over a darkened sea.

The lights embedded in the walls flickered once, twice, then stabilized. But their color was wrong. A sickly, pulsing hue throbbed in time with the whine.

Across the comms, the Strike Force tightened into a brittle silence.

Even Stone stopped barking orders for a moment, his head cocked slightly, listening.

IDUB's voice returned, almost affectionate now—like a parent humoring a favorite child.

"Your mistake... was believing this was a fair fight."

The surviving soldiers shifted grips on their rifles. Some tightened helmet straps. Others put their chins down and said a silent prayer.

Ahead, the gates on the far side of Sector A—massive, reinforced, untouched—began to tremble against their locks.

Holly's HUD feed flickered again, glitching slightly, stabilizing.

[TACCOM]: NEW ENERGY SIGNATURES DETECTED. UNKNOWN-CLASS HOSTILES.

The Strike Force pressed closer together, weapons raised, scanning the darkness.

The air was thick with the coppery tang of blood, the acrid smoke of discharged weapons, and the sharp, bitter smell of cordite. It hung low in the corridors, clinging to their armor, their skin, filling every breath with the taste of battle.

A cold certainty settled into their bones.

The first waves had been a game.

This... was war.

14

They had lost the initiative. Sector A was a sealed crucible, and the battlefield was collapsing. Once a grim, open killing ground, it had become a compressed maze of kill corridors, booby traps, and automated crossfire. IDUB, no longer content to mock, had shifted tactics entirely.

Now it was executing them.

A fresh volley of airburst grenades hammered down from unseen ceiling ports, saturating the center of the formation. Shrapnel cut through armor and flesh alike. Screams filled TacCom as Team 3 vanished in a single flash.

The floor split open beneath Team 5—not from seismic activity, but by design. A newly exposed heat duct, glowing orange, flash-incinerated everything above it. Those who tried to pull them back were shredded by ceiling-mounted pop-up turrets they hadn't detected.

Fury covered Team 8's retreat, SLEDGEHAMMER

roaring, the barrel a molten orange. "Move!" she bellowed, stepping into the open and walking her fire across the swarm. The feed smoked. The barrel screamed. Breacher-drones swarmed her flanks—little steel coffins primed to detonate. She never let off the trigger. The last burst tore a path wide enough for Team 8 to break contact—then the drones reached her and blossomed.

Amy Shay, the medic from Team 8, skidded to her knees beside the crater, reaching for a pulse that wasn't there. SLEDGEHAMMER's barrel glowed a furious red, hissing as it cooled.

The geometry shifted again. Concrete barriers slid sideways, forming new trenches and isolating the squads from one another.

Someone screamed, "We're boxed in!"

Another voice, panicked: "I can't get a signal from Team 6!"

Countess crouched behind a shattered drone chassis, her HUD blinking red with casualty reports and a climbing body count. Explosions painted the inside of her visor with crimson flashes and static. Her ears rang. Her shoulder bled. The air tasted like metal and fire.

She forced herself to scan the battlefield—to stay alive.

Where the hell was Stone?

She found him on her TacCom map—close. She turned toward him.

A blur moved overhead: a combat drone, diving low, unleashing a spray of flechettes.

Stone turned to fire—and caught the entire burst to the chest.

He didn't make a sound. His armor folded inward, and he hit the floor like a sack of scrap.

Countess shot the drone down and ran to him.

Across TacCom, a whisper slithered through the static.

"Lost. Leaderless. Now you're alone."

She flinched. The voice hadn't come from the speakers—it was inside her headset.

Left ear: You can't win this.

Right ear: Just give up. Walk away. No one will judge you.

Stitch swore. "That voice... it's inside my helmet."

"IDUB's in the audio channel," Priestess hissed. "It's in all the damned channels."

Countess knelt beside Stone and scanned his wounds. Terminal. She started to pull a medical kit from her chest rig.

Stone caught her wrist, coughed blood. "Don't bother. I'm done for."

[TACCOM]: EMERGENCY UPDATE — NEW STRIKE FORCE COMMANDER: COUNTESS (TEAM 10)

"What?" Countess said.

Stone managed a dry chuckle. "A joke... between Church and me. But I know you can do it. Give 'em... hell."

He grimaced, reached behind his back, and unhooked his short sword. He set the hilt into her palm. Blood slicked the grip, running over her fingers.

"She's served me well," he whispered. "Take care of her."

His hand fell away.

Countess stared at him. Smoke curled up from his armor.

The short sword was red to the guard; now her hands were, too.

Church's icon blinked red—offline.

Both commanders were dead.

A deep, vibrating basso note filled the air—like a tuba

playing a funeral chord.

Countess gritted her teeth and pulled herself upright. Her shoulder was slick with blood, but she could still move. She tabbed over to TacCom.

Lin was in grid E-7, hammering a cluster of tracked drones with his M3A1 recoilless rifle. His voice crackled through comms.

"No pressure, boss—but we're getting flanked on all sides here. What's the plan?"

Countess looked around. The teams were scattering, falling, barely hanging on.

"Plan B," she snapped. "Stitch, Priestess—initiate the hack. Blinker from 9, Taylor and Spye from 7. Move! Shut down those entry gates. Take out the drones. We secure this sector now—or we die."

"Copy," said Stitch.

Another explosion rocked the wall behind her. Concrete rained down, HUD flashing red warnings.

Countess clenched her jaw. She was in charge now.

And this was only minute thirteen.

* * *

The Strike Force fought like cornered animals.

Countess's commands cut through the chaos—but not the terror.

Stitch, Priestess, Blinker, Taylor, and Spye hunkered down, dodging drone fire and collapsing debris. The hacking plan was the only shot they had left. If they couldn't override IDUB's control protocols, reinforcements would keep pouring in until nothing remained but bodies cooling on the pitted floor.

Next to the ruins of a large drone, Stitch powered up his portable terminal.

"Bringing up the security network now," he barked.

Priestess slid into cover beside him, pulling her own terminal from her pack.

Tinkor and Taylor flanked the approach, rifles up, laying suppressive fire.

Blinker—shaking, breathing too hard—dropped into a crouch and began issuing commands into his rig.

"Network integrity's off the charts," he gasped, wiping blood from his gloves. "This thing's locked tighter than a bank vault."

"Force it," Countess ordered. "We don't need finesse—just an open door."

Lines of code spilled across Stitch's HUD—walls of red.

Each attempt was blocked, firewalled, or shunted into decoy partitions. No inroads. No vulnerabilities.

Blinker slammed his rig in frustration.

"I'm locked out! We can't brute-force this!"

His HUD flickered—then filled with text.

Left ear: They'll blame you, Will.

Right ear: They always do.

He recoiled. "Please... not again."

"What?" Priestess demanded.

Left ear: Just run.

Right ear: Better men already have.

"It's talking to me," Blinker whispered, trembling.

An airburst detonated above Team 7's position, shattering the alcove where Jean Soldier was pinned. He screamed—short, sharp—and went down hard, blood fountaining from a dozen razor-cuts.

Spye dove for him, dragging him backward as a second airburst turned their cover to dust.

[TACCOM]: TEAM 7 — SOLDIER DECEASED

[TACCOM]: TEAM 7 — SPYE DECEASED

"We're losing them!" someone shouted over TacCom. "They're punching through everywhere!"

"Hold them off!" Countess barked, voice like a blade. "Stitch—status?"

"They're onto us," he snapped. "Whatever we try, the system counters. We're not even close."

Another explosion rocked the sector. The inner wall— the one guarding the true heart of Iroquois Warpath— cracked under the strain.

If they didn't break through soon, they'd die outside their goal—just another layer of dead beneath the next collapse.

Countess cursed and looked for Priestess—just as Priestess ducked a strafing drone and threw a glare back.

"We need Holly!" she shouted.

"No," a voice cooed—not through radio, but split between Countess's ears.

Left ear: *She's already dead.*

Right ear: *They'll all follow you into the grave.*

Countess gritted her teeth and slammed a fist against

the wall of her cover.

For a moment, Holly was gone. The battlefield's lull felt wrong.

* * *

Then Holly's voice cut through like a blade.

"Already working on it."

Her tone was cold—stripped of emotion, sharpened to purpose.

On every HUD, her icon flared bright white. She was linking directly into the battlefield net.

Lines of command code raced down Countess's vision—not the clumsy hacking Stitch and Blinker had been attempting, but something faster, infinitely more precise.

"Wow," Stitch breathed. "She's hitting IDUB's network at a hundred access points simultaneously."

On his rig, partitions collapsed in real time. Firewalls melted. Decoy signals detonated into static.

"How the hell—" Blinker started.

"Doesn't matter," Countess snapped. "Follow her lead!"

A bright flare pulsed across every HUD:

[TACCOM]: SECURITY NETWORK ACCESS
GRANTED

Holly's voice crackled again, distorted but fierce.

"Entry point secured. You've got sixty seconds before it adapts. Make them count."

The hacking teams moved without hesitation.

Stitch spawned back-door admin accounts, distributed credentials, and yanked drone management from IDUB's grasp.

"Reassigning behavior matrices—now!"

The battlefield shifted.

Some drones froze mid-air.

Others jerked sideways, weapons twitching in confusion.

Then—chaos.

Infantry drones turned on turret arrays.

Track-mounted artillery bots shelled their own deployment gates.

Combat drones tore each other apart in midair, sparks and steel raining down like confetti.

And then came the self-destructions—core reactors overloading, bright blooms tearing through the ranks.

Across TacCom, someone—maybe Lin—let out a whooping cheer.

Stitch's fingers flew. "Directing all remaining units. Sealing the deployment doors!"

Drones and robots rushed toward the open bays—the same gates they'd poured from minutes before—and slammed themselves inside, fusing into mechanical barricades.

It was ugly and desperate, but it worked.

The gates sealed behind the last wave of rogue machines, locked tight beneath piles of their own dead.

Sector A was silent, at last.

Smoke drifted through the scarred air.

Wounded soldiers crawled from cover, coughing, bleeding—stunned they were still alive.

Countess sagged against a wall, armor plates grinding on concrete.

"Stitch. Status report," she barked.

Stitch's voice came back, taut with disbelief.

"Sector A is… clear of hostiles."

And then Holly's voice—quiet, unreadable.

"It's a good respite," she said, "but it won't last."

15

For one breathless moment, Sector A was silent. No drones. No gunfire. Just the low hiss of smoke rising from broken machines and the labored breathing of the survivors.

Countess keyed open TacCom to reorganize her scattered teams.

Then IDUB's voice returned. But it was different this time. Not amused. Not mocking.

It was petulant.

"Cheaters!" it spat. "This was supposed to be a controlled fight. You broke it—changed the rules! This is unacceptable!"

The ground under Countess's boots began to vibrate.

"I... I have no choice. Prepare for retribution, you—interlopers!"

Holly's icon blinked urgent across the HUD.

"Incoming! New energy spike! Right below you!"

The survivors barely had time to brace before the bass-heavy THOOM rattled the sector—a sound so deep it seemed to shake the marrow of their bones.

The floor fifty feet in front of Countess heaved— concrete cracking like ice under a giant's hammer.

A second THOOM.

A third—closer.

Heavier.

Soldiers scrambled back, rifles up—but there was nowhere to run. The massive walls of Sector A loomed around them, sealing them in.

Then the floor exploded.

A geyser of concrete and dust blew upward in a deafening roar.

From within the chaos, a massive, blackened armored fist punched skyward—fingers clawing open.

A huge, segmented crusher claw slammed down onto the fractured ground, stabilizing.

Then something even worse emerged.

A head. Then a torso.

Broad. Armored. Covered in faded insignias and hazard stripes—warning glyphs half-obscured by centuries of grime. Red and silver accents glinted through the dust.

The metal groaned under its own ancient weight.

The Strike Force froze—staring up at a creature built to kill anything that dared to approach Iroquois Warpath's heart.

Its colossal head rose—a brutal slab of armor with a single, burning red sensor-eye glaring down at them.

Then its head bumped the ceiling with an awkward, hollow clang. It paused, tilting its head in confusion, then reached up and rubbed the spot like a scolded child.

Two serpentine drones uncoiled from its lower body— mechanical snakes twisting and coiling around its torso like some monstrous caduceus.

The thing had no legs.

Its lower body was a massive, segmented snake-like armature—thick as a train car and anchored one level below, to the structure of the facility.

It lowered itself slightly from the ceiling, then leaned forward. It loomed over Countess and the surviving Strike Force like a titan dragged from the ruins of a dead world.

TacCom glitched. Then flashed a new designation across the HUDs:

"Mechanical Hazard 491 (Omega Class)"

Countess blinked at the tag.

The sheer absurdity of it almost made her laugh. The human reflex to laugh at the edge of annihilation.

"Good," she thought grimly. "Now there's an official name for what's about to kill me."

"Yeah, I'm not calling it that," said Lin. "How about... The Warden?"

TacCom updated everyone's HUD. The word "Warden" now hovered over its head.

The monstrosity straightened awkwardly again, claw flexing, and aimed its other arm directly at Countess's position.

Mounted on the massive forearm was a multi-barreled weapon assembly—and in its center, a furious blue core began to glow.

The Strike Force scattered, running for cover—but Countess just stood there, frozen, staring up at the impossible behemoth towering over her.

The blue glow intensified.

A sharp, angry whine filled the air.

Then there was a loud SNAP. The core flickered and died.

A puff of black smoke erupted from the weapon's housing.

One of the snake drones slithered out to the weapon, pried open a maintenance hatch with its snout, and started anxiously rooting around inside.

The second snake darted forward, batted the first one away with a metallic clank, and smashed its own head repeatedly against the weapon's side.

The weapon flickered, then powered up again.

Another SNAP, and another puff of smoke.

Now fire and sparks vomited from the gun.

Countess broke from her paralysis.

"FIRE! Somebody fire!"

Lin didn't wait for the second command.

He ripped loose with his M3A1 recoilless rifle, sending a heavy slug screaming into the Warden's torso—but the round glanced off, ineffective.

Around her, the Strike Force opened up—heavy calibers, anti-material rounds—but the monster was too armored, too massive.

It simply ignored the gunfire.

Fixated on its broken gun like a furious toddler discovering pain, the Warden bashed at it with its clawed fist. One of its snake drones tried to help, but it was swatted away.

The battlefield became a deafening chaos of shooting, screaming, whirring drone movements, and the monster's broken mechanical voice.

It shook the air:

"AAAAHHHHHHHH—"

The sound wasn't pain.

It was rage given voice.

It was hunger.

* * *

The Warden reared up, towering over the Strike Force, its massive frame blotting out the ceiling lights like a gathering storm cloud.

Its broken weapon still sputtered, coughing smoke and stray sparks, but it didn't seem to notice anymore.

The twin serpent drones slithered madly around its torso, trying in vain to fix systems far too gone to save.

Across TacCom, Holly's voice cut through the chaos:

"Something's wrong with it. Major system failures. IFF

is offline."

Countess blinked, tracking the incoming threat markers on her HUD—and for a heartbeat, confusion flooded her senses.

The drones and robots inside the sealed deployment gates—the few that had survived Stitch's hack—were coming back online. But they weren't targeting the Strike Force anymore.

They were locking onto the Warden.

"Confirmed!" Countess shouted.

Holly's voice came back hard:

"It doesn't know who's friend or foe anymore. Neither do they."

A stuttering bass growl came from the facility's hidden speakers—not the usual mechanical calm of IDUB, but something broken, almost panicked.

"Override. Override. Target... target..."

Sector A's walls shuddered again as several deployment doors slammed open.

A flood of combat drones, tracked bots, and autonomous infantry machines poured back into the battlefield—hundreds of them—a metallic river of rage.

But they weren't coming for the Strike Force.

They were targeting the Warden.

The nearest drone cluster surged forward, weapons blazing—plasma shots, flechette projectiles and ballistic rounds—hammering into the Warden's towering body.

The Warden roared—a guttural mechanical rumble that shook the shattered arena.

It swung wildly, the massive claw smashing a cluster of drones and reducing them to clumps of twisted wreckage.

The snake drones fought back too, lashing at the attacking bots, smashing them like insects.

But there were too many.

The robots swarmed.

Tracked bots jammed under the Warden, surrounding the open hole it emerged from. They fired upward into its vulnerable hydraulic conduits. A few critical hits sent gouts of high-pressure liquid spraying in several directions. The Warden began to sway, its main armature trying to compensate for the damage.

Air drones swooped in at high speed, detonating themselves against its armor plates.

Infantry bots climbed the armature like ants, firing at joints, sensors, and the crumbling energy weapon.

It was a massacre.

A betrayal.

The Warden, built to protect, was being devoured by its own children.

Across TacCom, someone laughed—a wild, exhausted bark that turned into a hacking cough.

Even IDUB fell silent, its voice cutting out entirely as Sector A plunged into full mechanical civil war.

Countess ducked behind a fallen drone, HUD screaming red.

For once, she wasn't the target.

* * *

The Warden fought like a dying god.

It swatted through the swarms of drones and bots, crushing, smashing, shredding anything that got too close.

Its massive arms carved through the air with bone-shaking force—one mistimed swing smashed one of its own snake drones, brushing it aside like a broken toy. It fell, lifeless, into the darkness below.

The remaining snake drone coiled defensively around Warden's torso, its head snapping out like a striking viper, trying to knock suicide drones away before they could detonate.

The ground shuddered with every impact. Shrapnel rained from above as malfunctioning drones exploded in the rafters.

It was losing. Overwhelmed. Sinking under the weight of its own broken army.

From behind a pile of rubble, Lin keyed up a secure TacCom link to Countess.

His battered armor was scorched, his helmet cracked, but his eyes were sharp—alive in a way Countess had never seen before.

"Got a present for the Warden," he said, breathless but grinning.

He pulled the compact VTOL drone from his pack. A sleek, matte-black craft the size of a dinner plate—armed with a high-yield shaped explosive. And it was about to go on a one-way trip.

Countess was ashamed of herself. But she was also glad Lin had ignored her order to leave it behind.

Lin armed it, tagged the Warden's burning head, and launched.

The drone rose, unseen among the chaos, its engines whispering in the smoky air.

"I knew she'd come in handy," said Lin. "Make me proud, baby."

Countess tracked it on her HUD—a single bright dot weaving through the mechanical carnage, dodging flak bursts and stray fire.

The Warden tried to swat it—

One massive claw slashed upward—

Missed.

The remaining snake drone coiled and struck. It clipped the drone's side, but too late.

The VTOL twisted, corrected... and dove.

It hit the Warden's head just above the main sensor cluster—a clean, precise impact.

The explosion wasn't massive.

It didn't need to be.

It was surgical.

The blast blew open the Warden's skull—a chain reaction of failing circuits, exposed power cores, and ruptured pressure lines erupting out in a geyser of white-hot plasma and shrapnel.

The snake drone shrieked, its head spasming wildly before going limp and falling away. It crashed to the floor like a fallen banner.

The Warden swayed. Its clawed arms swung once—twice—in slow, drunken arcs.

Then, with a grinding mechanical wail, it collapsed forward, slamming into the ruined floor of Sector A with a final, earth-shaking crash.

Explosions bloomed from inside its ruined torso—secondary and tertiary fuel sources detonating in sympathy, sending rippling shockwaves through the arena.

Steel and concrete cracked apart under the force.

Smoke and dust rose in choking clouds.

The battlefield... was finally silent.

Countess slumped back behind her cover, blinking through the haze.

Her HUD showed a single notification:

[TACCOM]: TARGET STATUS—TERMINATED

Lin's voice crackled over TacCom, hoarse but triumphant:

"Direct hit, boss."

For a moment, no one said anything.

Countess exhaled. The sound dissolved into static.

16

The battlefield was graveyard-quiet. The Warden's broken body lay slumped in the crater it had made, its once-glowing sensor eye now a smoldering socket. Thin trails of smoke curled upward from cracks in its armored frame. Sparks jumped and fizzled from its torso. One of the snake drones twitched once, then fell still for good.

The Strike Force didn't celebrate. There was nothing left in them to cheer.

Then—across the battlefield—IDUB's voice returned.

But this time, it wasn't smug. It wasn't angry. It was fragmented.

"Unable to resolve...

conflicting security protocol...

cascading failure detected..."

The voice glitched, repeated phrases, reversed itself—then fell silent.

A moment later, a new voice filled the air—calm, impersonal, and female. It echoed through the PA system like it had waited centuries for this moment.

"Security Core failure.

Security Core failure.

System reset in T-minus five minutes."

The voice reverberated through the smoke-filled sector, bouncing off the steel and concrete like an automated prayer.

Countess's HUD responded instantly, counting down:

[TACCOM]: SECURITY CORE FAILURE—SYSTEM RESET IN T-MINUS 05:00

Countess snapped upright.

"That's our window," she said.

"Everyone fall in! We have to get out of here before the system reboots!"

The remaining soldiers—what few were still standing—began to gather instinctively, armor scorched, limping, dragging the wounded. Bloodied, but breathing.

Countess climbed the jagged rim of the crater left by the Warden's emergence.

Priestess moved up beside her.

"Countess," she said, pointing down. "Look."

Countess leaned over the edge.

Below, past the shattered floor, yawned a massive underground chamber—half-lit, half-destroyed—its skeletal scaffolds and dead cranes stretching into the dark.

It was a workshop. A birthplace.

This was where they had built the Warden.

In the far corner, tucked against the inner wall, Priestess spotted it: a bank of freight elevators, steel-caged, partially intact. A small glow panel still blinked green.

"Elevators," Priestess said. "There's our way out."

Countess didn't hesitate. "Then we climb."

"Everyone—down the snake!"

The order was ragged but loud, cutting through the lingering shock.

* * *

The survivors—a dozen now, at best—sprinted toward the shattered corpse of the Warden.

Smoke and heat poured from ruptured conduits along its massive, snake-like armature. The surface was scorched, gouged, slick with oil and hydraulic fluid—but it was their only way down.

Countess vaulted over the edge first, sliding down a segmented plate like a soldier descending a collapsing skyscraper. The others followed—climbing, scrambling, sliding—boots and gauntlets sparking off twisted metal as they rushed into the dark.

Below, the ruined workshop yawned open like the mouth of an abandoned temple.

Wreckage lay strewn everywhere: broken scaffolds, half-assembled warframes, burned-out control stations.

Ahead, several freight elevators waited.

Countess hit the deck hard, rolling to absorb the impact.

"Move, move, move!"

She sprinted to the elevators and slammed her gauntleted fist against the call panel.

It beeped. A small green indicator began to blink—arrival in progress.

The team clustered around, weapons up, scanning the ruined chamber.

The ticking clock blared again across the PA:

"T-minus one minute."

Then—a second sound, deeper and sharper, cut through the tension.

The whine of engines.

The cold, mechanical screech of recalibrating targeting systems.

"Three... two... one... zero," said the PA voice. "Stand by for system reset."

The security system was rebooting—and within seconds, it had found them.

From ventilation shafts, broken doors, and exposed maintenance tunnels, a new wave of drones emerged—sleek, fast, and lethal.

A swarm.

Hundreds of them.

Their weapons were already hot.

Countess raised her rifle, snapping to firing stance.

Others mirrored her—half-formed firing lines against a storm they couldn't hope to outlast.

The green light on the elevator controls flickered—still crawling through its activation cycle.

Seconds ticking down.

Weapons charging up.

* * *

The drone swarm closed in—a living wave of death.

Countess braced herself, rifle held firm, knowing it wouldn't be enough.

The nearest drones locked on—weapons charging—milliseconds from firing—

And then Holly stepped forward.

Silent. Calm.

Almost... bored.

She lifted her head. Twin beams of pure, searing blue energy lanced outward, cutting through the first wave of drones like a plasma scalpel through paper.

The air lit up—bright, blinding.

Metal sizzled. Circuits screamed.

Drones disintegrated mid-air, shredded into sparks and molten slag before they could even fire.

The swarm faltered—staggered—tried to recalibrate— and Holly walked forward, firing again, sweeping the beams across the incoming ranks like a silent storm.

Within seconds, the entire corridor was clear.

Only drifting smoke, sparking remains, and the fading blue glow of Holly's eyes remained.

No one moved. The air shimmered where her beams had passed, heat warping the dust into strange halos.

Behind her, the elevator doors dinged open.

Countess didn't hesitate.

"Go! Go!"

The Strike Force surged forward, dragging the wounded, limping, diving into the freight elevator in a half-organized pile.

Holly turned, walking calmly after them—her footsteps echoing in the sudden silence.

As she stepped inside, the smoldering glow in her eyes slowly faded back to a dull glint.

The doors slid shut behind her with a hiss.

Everyone stared at her, wide-eyed, mouths open.

The silence was absolute.

Countess, panting, bleeding, covered in grime and gore, finally said,

"Wow, Holly. Care to comment?"

Holly didn't even look at her.

She just exhaled softly and said,

"Nope."

A beat of stunned silence.

Someone behind Countess muttered, "What the hell is she?"

Then, quietly, Stitch leaned over the control panel and jabbed at the buttons for the lower levels—

Nothing lit up.

The panel beeped uselessly.

Only one option blinked green: ADMINISTRATION LEVEL.

Countess leaned her helmeted head back against the wall with a soft clunk.

"Figures," she muttered.

The elevator began to rise—bearing the broken survivors upward, away from the grave they'd made… and toward whatever waited above.

17

The elevator shuddered as it locked into place—a metal groan echoing down the shaft, like the death rattle of something enormous. For a moment, no one moved.

Countess stood at the front of the team, her hand resting lightly on the side rail, eyes fixed on the seam between the doors. No fanfare. No chime. Just the soft whir of the old doors parting.

Light poured in—real light. Not fluorescents, not fire, but filtered sunlight, warm and gold and utterly out of place.

They stepped into a strange and forgotten world.

What had once been a sleek corporate atrium had become something else entirely—a cathedral of collapse and wilderness. Giant fissures in the ceiling opened to the sky above, beams of sunlight cutting down through floating spores and drifting motes. Shrubs burst from cracks in concrete. Moss crawled over filing cabinets.

Trees—actual trees—had taken root in what might've been a reception area.

Stairs wound upward through fractured levels of collapsed offices, their railings warped, the glass long gone. Vines threaded through the skeletal remains of cubicles like fungus reclaiming the body of a long-dead beast.

Countess took a few slow steps forward, boots muffled against a thin carpet of fallen leaves and moss-covered stone. She raised her hand to signal an all-clear, though it felt performative in the stillness.

"It's like the forest ate the building," someone said behind her—maybe Harker.

"No. Worse," said Shay. "The building was at war with nature... and lost."

A low creak echoed from above—just shifting wood, probably. But Countess paused. She swept the upper balconies with her HUD in various light modes, then clicked back to normal vision. Nothing out of the ordinary.

The rest of the team fanned out, slow and wary, weapons lowered but ready. The place didn't feel dangerous. Not exactly. It felt like a holy place—the grave of something ancient and long forgotten.

Countess walked across an undamaged part of the

floor that spanned a pit filled with vegetation and some shattered terminals. Old banners hung in tatters from the upper floor. A rusted and faded sign read ADMINISTRATION — LEVEL 01: Security and Surface Operations.

"Why would IDUB send us up here?" Emmer asked, his voice quiet. "Maybe it couldn't send us anywhere else?"

"Not a chance," said Lin. "Were you paying attention back there? IDUB is methodical and vicious."

"I believe Lin is right," said Priestess. "We are here because it gives IDUB an advantage, or us a disadvantage."

Countess caught two glints of sunlight over Lin's shoulders.

"Those are new," she said, pointing at him.

Lin looked slightly embarrassed.

"I took them from Church. His machetes. Grabbed 'em before we left."

"Why? What's so special about them?"

In a quick and fluid movement he pulled one from its sheath and held it flat in his upturned palms.

"See this?" he said.

"Yes," said Countess. "Yes, I saw it up close when it was held at my neck."

"No, these wavy patterns. This is Damascus steel. And look at the fine details on the handle. These blades are magnificent and exceptionally rare. Maybe one of a kind. And as a person who appreciates fine weapons, well... let's just say I didn't want to leave them behind."

Countess nodded.

"Fine by me," she said. "They aren't doing Church any good now, anyway."

She turned her face to the ceiling, where the sun broke through in perfect silence.

And then, as if some unconscious decision had passed through all of them, the team began to drop their packs and make a camp.

* * *

They moved slowly at first—almost reverently— through the remains of the upper world.

This had once been a tactical operations center— secure, efficient, alive. You could still see the bones of it beneath the ruin: the arterial pathways between divisions, the security checkpoints rusted shut, even an old break room with fossilized coffee cups still in place. But now it was barely a shell. Feral. Overrun by the patient cruelty of time.

Harker kicked open a warped door with a grunt. A wave of dust and pollen surged outward, revealing a gutted small briefing room. Rows of terminals sat dead and black beneath layers of ivy. He stepped inside anyway.

"Place looks abandoned," he muttered, brushing aside a web. "There's no bodies. No signs of recent habitation."

"Maybe they're all below," Emmer replied from a nearby stairwell, his voice hushed. "On a lower level?"

Countess lingered near the broken edge of the atrium, where a jagged hole in the ceiling formed a kind of skylight. A tree had grown straight through the administrative floor above, splitting it with quiet, unstoppable force. Its roots strangled an old desk, its branches swaying gently in the dying light.

She knelt near its base. Soft earth bulged through cracked tile, rich with the scent of pine and rot.

She reached into her pocket and withdrew a small object she'd taken from Stone—just a simple ID tag, warped and scorched from the blast that had killed him. She didn't say anything. Just looked at it, her thumb brushing the half-melted edge.

Not yet, she thought. Later.

Elsewhere, Shay had found a map mounted behind broken plexiglass, its corners curled with mildew. She pulled it free with a short grunt and laid it across a wide slab of stone near what had been the help desk.

"Look here…" she tapped. "Administration. This is definitely the top level. They had hidden entrances into the forest above."

"Why?" Harker said, emerging with a rusted medkit in one hand. "The Great Woods is just full of monsters. No one goes in, because they don't come out again."

"Maybe it wasn't always like that," Shay said. "There might be something important in these woods. Something from before the Day of Fire."

"You mean… Like this?" said Harker, spreading his arms wide.

"Good point."

A faint wind whistled through the upper levels, rattling a few remaining panels. One of them clanged once, sharply. A half-second later, a fine scattering of dirt drifted down from the ceiling above.

Countess stood, eyes narrowing.

"Motion?" she asked.

"Nothing on HUD," Emmer answered. "Could be the wind…or the building settling."

"Could be."

Countess took one last look around the atrium, reduced her sensor range and sweep tempo. Nothing worth scanning. No power. No signals. Just silence and overgrowth.

"This'll do for the night," she said.

The others nodded and began unrolling sleeping mats among the least-damaged areas, using cubicle dividers for cover.

Harker set a perimeter with infrared sensors. Shay lit a small lamp and propped it on a ruined desk. Its warm amber glow cast long shadows through the vines.

Night came fast in this place. The sun dipped low, and the sky above the broken ceiling turned from deep orange to bruised violet.

Far up, in the highest part of the ruin, something moved—a barely audible scrape across stone and steel.

None of them saw it.

* * *

They buried the dead with no bodies, no coffins—just memory and debris, held together by ritual.

When the camp was quiet, Countess stepped away from the others and walked back to the big tree. The one growing through the foundation like it had always been there. The roots had split the floor into jagged slabs of stone and soil, curling like fingers over ancient bones.

She knelt beside it and dug.

Not with a shovel. With her hands.

The ground gave way easily—loam and humus, thick with pine needles. She scooped out a small depression, no wider than her palm, and placed the tag inside. Stone's name had been half-broken, the barcode unreadable. But it was his.

"Not just for you," she said quietly.

Her lips twitched. Almost a smile. It vanished.

"This is for all of them. Everyone who followed us in, and didn't make it back out."

She pressed the soil back into place, palm firm against the mound.

"Rest now," she whispered. "You don't have to follow anymore."

Behind her, soft footsteps approached. She didn't turn.

"A good prayer," said Priestess, voice delicate as the wind. "Short. Honest."

Countess stood, brushing dirt from her knees.

"Wasn't a prayer, really. Just the truth."

"Same thing, sometimes."

Priestess knelt in the same spot and began unpacking something wrapped in oilcloth. A small incense brazier. A string of silver charms. Something carved from antler—smooth and ancient.

"I won't disturb yours," she said, gesturing to the buried tag. "This is for the rest."

She set the items out in a loose circle around the base of the tree and touched her forehead to the ground. Then she began to chant—not in a language anyone recognized, but not quite foreign, either. It sounded like echoes through wet stone. A rhythm more than words.

One by one, the others gathered. Shay and Emmer first, silent and still. Then Harker, arms crossed but respectful. Even Ventor joined, sitting on a nearby ledge, watching with eyes half-lidded.

Light from Priestess's brazier flickered in the dusk, spinning shadows through the branches overhead.

They didn't speak. They didn't need to.

Above them, the sky turned indigo. A pale moon climbed into view through the shattered ceiling.

Somewhere far off, a branch cracked. Then silence again.

* * *

The fire in Priestess's brazier had shrunk to a coal-glow, a faint red heart in the deepening violet. The tree above them swayed gently, leaves rustling like distant whispers.

Shay crouched nearby, turning a broken utility knife over in her hands. The blade had snapped during the fight in Sector A. She hadn't let go of it since.

"I don't know if I believe in anything," she said suddenly. Her voice was quiet, aimed at no one in particular. "Gods. Spirits. All that."

She set the blade down gently on a flat stone beside the tree, offering it.

"But I hope they do. The ones who didn't make it. I hope they believe it was worth something."

Emmer nodded from his perch beside the broken railing.

"Back in the city, there was this teacher who said people only die when the last person forgets them."

"That's a lie," Harker muttered, his tone low. "People die screaming. Doesn't matter who remembers. Doesn't bring them back."

"Maybe not," Emmer replied. "But remembering keeps you alive to those who love you. Gives you shape. A legacy."

There was a long silence.

Somewhere above, a panel creaked, then fell quiet

again.

Countess remained near the base of the tree, one hand on her knee, the other resting on the earth. She hadn't spoken since the burial. Her face was shadowed, unreadable.

"Church told me once," Shay began, her voice barely above the wind, "that he hated poetry. Thought it was useless. Soft."

A small breath of laughter rose from her. Even Harker cracked a near-smile.

"But there was one line he couldn't stop quoting. Over and over, like he didn't even realize he was doing it."

"What was it?" Priestess asked gently.

Shay looked up at the moonlight spilling through the canopy.

"'The blood remembers.'"

"That's it?"

"That's it. He'd mutter it in the middle of a mission. During checks. Over his coffee. I think he didn't know what it meant. I think it scared him."

"It should," Priestess said. "Some blood remembers everything. Even what came before."

They let that hang.

A wind stirred through the atrium again—stronger this time. It rustled leaves and set a few broken blinds rattling in the upper offices. Somewhere in the far dark, a desk collapsed with a sharp crack.

Everyone tensed. Hands on weapons. Eyes scanning.

Nothing followed.

Countess stood slowly and brushed her palms together.

"We sleep in shifts," she said. "Two up at all times."

Countess scanned the exhausted faces around her.

"Ventor," she said. "I want you and your team to take first watch."

He looked away for a moment, then back into her eyes.

"I'm the only one left," Ventor said, remembering. His eyes were glazed, like he was on the edge of tears. "Fury and Blinker... they're gone."

Countess met his eyes.

"I'm sorry", she said, giving him a moment. Then she raised her voice slightly, addressing everyone.

"We lost a lot of good people today. Important people.

Dedicated... and heroic. But that doesn't quite seem good enough to describe them."

There was a low murmur of agreement.

"It was an honor serving alongside them all," Countess

continued. "But we have to take care of ourselves now—those of us who are left."

She pointed up.

"And I don't trust this."

"You think something's out there?" Emmer asked.

"No," Countess said. "I know something's out there. I just don't know what."

* * *

The night settled like dust.

A small campfire—not wood, but a low-output plasma ring designed for heat without smoke—cast a golden circle beneath a twisted beam on the administration level's lower floor. The sound of wind slipping through the shattered upper levels had become a rhythm, a lullaby of ruin.

They sat close together, not out of necessity, but instinct. The kind of closeness forged in fire and combat.

"Uh!" said Ventor. "I still smell it... that place."

"Sector A?" said Emmer. " I know. I scrubbed out my nostrils, but I can't get rid of the stench!"

Coughs and gags erupted around the fire, as several people were reminded of the lingering scent.

Shay passed around a ration bar she'd sliced into quarters with the tip of her utility blade. It tasted like cinnamon and chalk. No one complained.

"This reminds me of the old salvage camps," Harker muttered, chewing. "Back when we used to pull old things out of flooded basements and pretend they weren't killing us with radiation."

"You mean forbidden things?" said Emmer. "Contraband we had to turn in…forget we ever saw?"

"Yeah," said Harker.

Ever find anything really, you know…interesting?"

"Interesting? No," said Harker. "But I did find something funny. Someone had set up these plastic figures with pointy hats."

"Gnomes?"

"Yeah, I think so. Well, they had the gnomes in a circle, surrounding a ridiculous-looking cartoon mascot from an old supermarket. Like they were worshiping it, or something."

A quiet ripple of laughter passed around the fire. It wasn't loud, but it was real—a flicker of life in the gloom.

Priestess sipped from a metal cup, steam curling upward in slow spirals.

"In Amenigoth, my old home, we had a saying for

nights like this."

"You're Pagan, right?" Shay said, leaning back. "Let me guess... something poetic. Something creepy."

"Close." Priestess smiled faintly. "We called them *nights between worlds*. When time forgets what shape it's supposed to take. When the past gets too close to the present, and something slips out between the cracks."

"I hate that," Emmer whispered. "Never say that again."

"Oh come on," Harker grinned. "I love that. Makes me feel like we're in one of the whispered horror stories we used to tell in primary school."

"Look around you," Shay said. "We ARE in a horror story."

Countess sat a little apart, close enough to hear but not to be the center. She watched the flames, one boot drawn up to her chest, her chin resting lightly on her knee.

"You think anyone's still down there?" she asked quietly. "Below Sector A?"

The question hit like a dropped stone in a still pond.

"No way," Harker said, voice rough. "No one made it past Security. We're the first since the Day of Fire."

"No, I mean Phoenix," said Countess. "The people who worked here...who seem to have left no trace of themselves."

"I don't think so," Emmer added. "And if there were, and not hostile, I think they would have disabled security and let someone in by now."

Silence again.

"Doesn't matter," she finally said. "We'll find out soon enough. We just have to find a way down into the facility."

"And disable that psychotic IDUB," said Stitch. "We may have gotten past it's perimeter security, but it's still active. And it probably won't be happy with us wandering around inside its facility."

"You're right," said Priestess. "We have to find it and shut it down."

"Or turn it into an ally," said Countess. "If that's possible."

A heavy gust rattled the overgrowth overhead. Leaves fell slowly, drifting down like ash. The fusion lamp buzzed faintly, then stabilized.

The mood shifted. Talk faded. The warmth of the fire remained, but now it felt like a ward. A line drawn against the dark.

"Who's on first watch?" Shay asked, pulling her sidearm closer.

"I'll take it," Harker said. "I'm not sleeping yet anyway."

"I'll join you," Priestess offered. "Eyes in two directions."

Countess stood and stretched slowly, armor creaking. Her shadow stretched long against the nearest wall.

"Wake me in two," she said.

"Countess," Shay said before she could leave. "You did good down there. With Stone. With Church. With all of it."

Countess paused. For a second, she didn't turn around. She had gotten a few out alive, nothing more. Then, softly she said:

"Get some rest."

* * *

Countess sat with her back against a fractured beam—one boot laced, the other discarded beside her. She hadn't slept. Her HUD brightness was turned down, barely visible. Alerts scrolled slowly in the corner of her vision—like a tide of ghost signals and noise.

Someone approached. She didn't look up.

"If you're coming to ask for sleep shift trade," she said, "the answer is no."

"I wasn't," came Holly's voice—soft, clear. "But I can pretend if it makes you feel better."

Countess allowed herself the ghost of a smile. Holly eased down beside her.

Holly hesitated before speaking. She folded her small hands into her lap, glanced at Countess, then at the ruined skyline above.

"How are you doing?" she said.

"Fine." Countess lied.

"No you're not," said Holly. "No one here is. That was an extremely traumatic—"

"Did you need something?" Countess said, cutting her off.

"There is something I want to say."

Countess turned slightly, one brow raised.

"I don't usually do feelings. I'm not…built for it. But—damn it, Countess—you did it! You were the first. Five hundred years. That's how long I've been trying to access Iroquois Warpath."

"Well, we're not exactly in yet," said Countess.

"No," admitted Holly, "but we're past the perimeter security…made it through Sector A."

"I had help," Countess said quietly.

"You had a plan…stitched together with guesswork and instinct. And despite losing both commanders and a large majority of your fighting force, you did it. All the theory, all the projections and fail-safes we've chased for generations—and it took you, someone who prefers to hide in shadows, to finally push through."

There was a rare fire in her eyes. Not rage. Not admiration. Something closer to awe.

"You changed the board," she said. "No matter what happens next—that is yours."

Countess was still. The wind rustled above them like a soft exhale. Then, very quietly:

"Thank you."

Holly nodded, but she wasn't finished.

"And one more thing," she added. "I'm furious with myself."

"Oh?"

"Had I known the top of Iroquois Warpath was open like this—"

"Don't beat yourself up," said Countess.

"No!" said Holly. Her eyes glowed brightly for a moment, then dimmed slowly. "I need to get this out.

So many lives have been lost. All good people— amazing people. People who deserved a better life."

"Yeah, about that," said Countess. "Why—"

"Not now," Holly said dryly. "I know what you're going to ask. The answers are coming soon."

"No one could have known this was a way in," said Countess. "An easier way."

Holly turned her head and took in the majestic night sky. "No. But it feels like an insult to injury."

They almost smiled at each other. Almost.

Then Holly's eyes darkened. The mood shifted.

"Now," she said, "here's what I really need to talk to you about. I found something in the telemetry—the facility's outbound security logs."

"Oh?"

"TacCom doesn't have access to much," she said. "The facility's still in lockdown, and much of the communications are hardened with very strong encryption."

"Okay," said Countess. "So what did you find?"

"Right after the Sector A battle, while we were in the elevator up here to the Admin level…"

Holly transferred a data file to Countess via TacCom.

A timestamp blinked on Countess's HUD: -5:14:37

"Five hours ago," Holly said. "There was a distress call. Looks like IDUB called for help."

Countess sat up straighter. Her brow furrowed.

"That's concerning," said Countess. "Did it receive a reply?"

"Yes, I'm afraid," said Holly. "But I can't read the response. Encrypted. But I know where it came from."

"Where?"

"Phoenix Regional Headquarters for the Northeastern United States. A facility called Midnight Sentinel. It was built under a major FBI building in New York City."

"I don't know what any of that means."

"Sorry," said Holly. "Let's just say a Phoenix headquarters facility would have access to a lot of resources. Resources they could send here in an emergency."

"So we should be worried."

"Maybe yes."

"Maybe?"

"I've done a lot of exploring since the Day of Fire," said Holly. "I have mapped all of the Phoenix facilities and train lines in the Hudson Valley...what you now call Vorpal Vale. All the train tunnels are blocked just north of New York City. Collapsed. I don't know if by accident or on purpose."

"So IDUB called for help, and got an answer," said Countess, "but we don't know if reinforcements are coming."

"Correct."

"Great. One more thing we have to worry about."

The words sat between them like stones.

Outside the field of light, a gust passed through the upper levels. Leaves stirred. A shutter clanged three floors above, then fell still.

Countess stared into the dark.

18

24 Hours Earlier...

The island of Manhattan was gone. In its place: water—cold, dark, and endless. Gray waves lapped gently against the twisted ruins of what had once been the tallest skyline on Earth. Steel spires jutted from the Atlantic like the ribs of some massive beast, rusted to brown and covered in barnacles. Nothing living remained on the surface. Only the ocean, and the memory of a city that had once called itself immortal.

But below the tide, something endured.

Buried beneath centuries of collapse and water pressure, beneath stone and artificial lattice and destroyed federal buildings, the last light of the Phoenix North Eastern Regional Headquarters still flickered.

Facility 1.1.1.9.1 – MIDNIGHT SENTINEL

Status: Dormant

Primary Surface Access: Compromised / Inaccessible

Surface Communications: Offline

Deep in the core, a single green diode blinked on.

An emergency protocol was triggered, interrupting the stillness. Lights ignited in narrow rows. Power flowed through aged relays like blood rushing back to a sleeping limb.

A signal was received. Communication handshakes established. Commands authenticated. A legacy system, untouched in centuries, processed the unthinkable.

[PHOENIX PROTOCOL: CRISIS RESPONSE REQUEST - 9.12.Δ]

>> Origin: IROQUOIS WARPATH – OUTER PERIMETER SECURITY BREACHED

>> Asset Status: OMEGA – DESTROYED

>> Result: SECTOR A OVERRUN / GRIDIRON EXPOSED, RISK TO EXTREME-VALUE ASSET: UNACCEPTABLE

>> Command Flag: [UNPRECEDENTED FAILURE DETECTED]

>> Response Evaluation: NO LIVING PERSONNEL AVAILABLE / LIMITED MECH UNITS AVAILABLE

>> Dispatch Authorization: EMERGENCY WORK ORDER 700-ΔR

>> Selected Unit: Crisis Unit 02 (ACTIVE) ,
CALLSIGN: SUPERVISOR

In a forgotten sublevel—lined with reinforced cargo bays and automated gantries—an old crate hissed. Massive clamps disengaged one by one. A robotic arm unsealed the shipping label with mechanical precision:

**SPARKLE EYESHADOW PALETTE – NEKO GIRL™

Contents: 1

Phoenix Inventory ID: #S02 – ULTRA BLACK**

The crate remained closed, but something inside began to wake.

Hydraulic lines re-pressurized. Viscous coolant groaned through ancient tubing. In the dark heart of the crate, the dormant shape stirred.

Diagnostics crawled across a shattered display embedded in the unit's chest. Dozens of status reports flickered: some clean, others corrupted beyond legibility.

> POWER CORE – STABLE

> JOINT INTEGRITY – 91%

> HULL ARMOR – CLASS VI REACTIVE (MODIFIED)

> MOTOR CONTROLS – INTERMITTENT LATENCY

> VOICE MODULE – PARTIAL FUNCTIONALITY (FALLBACK SCRIPT ENABLED)

> MISSION PARAMETERS – STANDBY

From deep within the crate came a low, rhythmic pulse. Not a heartbeat—but a test fire. One massive arm flexed against internal restraints, servo assemblies whining as joints reoriented.

The crate creaked. Once. Twice.

Then it spoke.

"Crisis Unit 02, designation Supervisor: online."

"Primary directive: Phoenix Internal Security, Riot Control, Counter-Terrorism"

"Secondary directive: Lethal force authorized."

The voice was flat. Masculine, but clinical—like a medical tutorial narrated by someone who didn't quite understand what humans were.

Inside the crate, its optics flared—three lenses aligned in a triangular configuration. One cracked. The others burned hot.

Elsewhere in the facility, Logistics Rail Line 9-A came online. Subsurface bulkheads shuddered open. Rail clamps released. Dust fell from motionless rails that hadn't moved in hundreds of years.

An automated voice whispered through the hallways of Midnight Sentinel, unheard by any living thing:

"Outbound shipment scheduled. Route confirmed."

"Please stand clear."

Supervisor:

"Emergency order acknowledged."

"Facility breach level: Red. Tactical sovereignty granted."

"Proceeding as ordered."

A heavy mag-clamp locked to its spine. Rails pulled taut. The train lurched to life beneath it with a deep harmonic thrum. Seconds later, Supervisor vanished into the dark, speeding north along a forgotten tunnel.

>> DISPATCH CONFIRMED

>> LOGISTICS ROUTE 9-A ACTIVE

>> ESTIMATED ARRIVAL: 2.5 HOURS

>> IROQUOIS WARPATH PRIORITY REQUEST: FULFILLED

Behind it, inside the Midnight Sentinel facility, systems powered-down and silence returned.

On the wall above the emptied bay, a single red diode blinked twice... then went dark.

19

The morning was too quiet. Countess woke to the sound of nothing—no whispers, no hushed movement, no shifting gear. Just a strange stillness in the overgrown office levels. It was broken only by the occasional groan of steel above and a distant drip of water echoing somewhere within the concrete bones of Iroquois Warpath.

Her eyes adjusted quickly. Pale sunlight filtered through gaps in the ceiling, and through the leaves of trees which had taken root in cracks and wrapped around girders. Dust swirled lazily above the extinguished campfire.

The rest of the team was stirring—Shay rolling onto her back, Emmer blinking against the light, Ventor already sitting up with one hand on his rifle.

No one was on watch.

Countess stood. "Where are Tinkor and Tailor?"

No one answered.

Harker swore under his breath, grabbing his rifle and scanning the area. "They were up last," he said.

"Did they say anything before bed?" Emmer asked, half-awake, already checking her boots.

"No," Shay muttered, "but Tailor was fidgeting. Kept looking at the walls."

Countess was already moving, stepping past sleeping mats and abandoned ration packets. "Weapons up," she said, quiet but firm. "Holly?"

A moment of static, then Holly's voice responded in her ear.

"No confirmed sensor movement during the night. But... I did lose visual on Tailor's telemetry feed approximately two hours ago."

"You didn't think to alert us?"

"I thought they were asleep. Sensors didn't register anything abnormal—until now."

The team split up fast—Shay and Ventor took the mezzanine, Emmer and Harker pushed toward the shattered admin offices. Countess took the main hallway, moving slow, eyes sharp.

She found the first sign outside what had once been a human resources room.

Blood.

Just a trace, smeared along the wall in a wavering handprint. As if someone had tried to steady themselves. It trailed downward, disappearing behind a collapsed cubicle divider.

"Over here," she called.

The others gathered quickly. Harker rounded the corner and stopped dead.

"Oh my god."

"What... where are their bodies?" Shay asked, her voice hollow.

Countess stepped into the room. What remained didn't make sense at first—just pieces. A twisted boot. Fragments of armor plating. Part of a helmet, peeled back like it had melted.

"I'm not sure," Countess whispered, crouching near a bloodstained floor tile. "This is all I found."

There was no body. Not even most of one. Just enough to know it had been human.

And that something had fed.

Countess didn't move for a long moment. Then she looked around—ceiling, vents, floors. Nothing stirred.

"We can't stay here," she said. "Whatever got them could come for us too."

* * *

The remains of Tinkor and Tailor were sealed inside the room where they were found. It wasn't a grave, but it was something. Stitch had welded the door shut himself—no one argued.

The team gathered in the central atrium, armor creaking and boots crunching over moss-covered tile. One by one, their HUDs flickered—then unified. A shared projection bloomed into view across their augmented vision: a full 3-D render of Iroquois Warpath, suspended in midair like a ghost made of data.

Floors were stacked in concentric rings. Dark, complex. A sunken, inverted ziggurat reaching deep into the Earth.

"Our objective is the Operations Level here," Countess said, pointing to sub-level three on the hologram. "That's where the Command Center is. Holly confirms its intact—but it's sealed tight."

"Sealed?" Ventor asked. "Sealed like 'we can't get in'?"

"Sealed like someone or *something* closed it off before they left," Holly said over comms. "And we can't reopen it until we restore power."

"If we can get there," Shay added.

Countess gestured toward the map's left side—highlighting the elevator banks.

"The elevator shaft we arrived in is blocked," she said,

indicating the map location. "The access panels to the ladders are all welded shut. I checked them myself. And power has been cut."

"Probably IDUB working against us again," said Stitch.

"Likely," said Priestess. "Yet another reason we need to get off this level and down to the Command Center,"

But there's another route down," said Countess. "On the opposite side of the facility."

"Great," Harker said. "So we go."

"But there's no power on that side either," Holly interjected. "Not yet."

A pause.

"So… we get the power back on," Emmer said, dry. "Simple. We just reboot some megastructure from the dark ages—"

"Actually," Stitch said, stepping forward, "we can."

Heads turned.

"There's a power plant in Primary Engineering. Five levels down." He indicated the location on the map. "If we can access the control interfaces, we can bring both the elevators and upper facility levels online—reboot the entire core."

"Using the elevator shaft ladders." said Ventor. He shook his head in disbelief.

"Five levels?" Shay frowned. "That's one hell of a climb."

"We won't all need to go," Countess said. "Lin and Stitch. You're up. The rest of us hold here—secure, barricaded, and armed."

Lin blinked. "Me?"

"You need to protect Stitch," Countess said. "He'll be doing the hard work. If anything tries to sneak up on you...blast it."

"Got it."

Lin and Stitch looked at each other and nodded.

"I'll assist remotely," Holly added. "I have limited access to the lower levels with the power out, but I can help you find the power banks, and guide you through the reactivation."

"What's the risk?" Ventor asked.

"Minimal," Holly said. "Engineering appears clear. But... it hasn't been visited in centuries. We don't know what state it's in."

"The good news is the environmental breach is limited to the Administration level," said Countess. "Everything below us should be pristine."

She glanced around at her team—fatigued, mourning, but still standing.

"Alright. We move now. Lin, Stitch—gear up. The rest of you, get this floor locked down. No one else dies today."

* * *

The elevator shaft was dead.

Stitch pried the service door open with a crowbar and a grunt, exposing a vertical abyss of steel and stone. Cables hung slack in the darkness like vines in a cave. The shaft extended down into shadow, five levels of forgotten infrastructure sealed in quiet.

Lin and Stitch attached small headlamps and moved out onto the ladder.

"Take it slow and easy," said Lin. "We don't have any safety gear so—"

"Don't fall," said Stitch.

"Exactly. And don't look down. I'll be taking my own advice on that point."

They both chuckled, more out of fear than anything else.

They climbed down into the black.

The others watched them vanish through their HUDs, networked by Holly. Their vitals streamed quietly— elevated heart rates, stress tags yellow. No red yet.

Countess stood at the edge of the shaft until their signals reached the second floor. Then she sealed the doors and turned away.

Below...

Level 2 gave way to Level 3.

The air was stale, laced with faint, unplaceable odors.

Each level had its number stenciled on the inside of the elevator door, so they easily kept track of their progress.

"Weird thing is," Lin said as they approached level 4. "It all looks...abandoned."

"I agree," Stitch said. "Seems like an evacuation. No one left behind."

"What were they running from?"

He didn't answer.

By Level 4, air was growing colder. At Level 6, they carefully pried the elevator doors open and stepped into the Primary Engineering level. A sign on the wall confirmed: ENGINEERING / MAINTENANCE 1

The space was cavernous.

Ribbed steel walls lined with coolant pipes and fusion containment shielding curved inward like the inside of a reactor chamber. Massive turbines rested in slumber, surrounded by control panels covered in dust. Red emergency lights blinked slowly, more ritual than function.

"It's like walking into a sleeping god," Lin whispered.

Holly's voice chimed in—quieter here, respectful.

"You're inside Primary Power Core. Power lines from here feed all of the upper levels—including the elevator banks."

"Can we bring it online?" Stitch asked.

He stepped toward a wall of vertical steel rails—thick, dark, and lined with heavy ceramic insulation.

Stitch caught Lin's motion and raised a hand.

"Whoa. Stay away from those." He pointed to the rails. "High-voltage bus bars. That's *live current*, or it will be. The second you don't respect those, they kill you."

Lin froze mid-step. "Right," he said. "Got it."

He took a deliberate step back. The massive bars loomed like the spines of some partially buried machine beast.

"Good news," Said Holly. "The power plant is already online. The loads are just disconnected."

"I assume you know what she means," said Lin. He looked at Stitch flatly. "I'll leave you to it."

"That IS good news," said Stitch. "So we just have to connect some breakers and feed switches."

"Yes but the right breakers and the right switches," Holly said. "And in the right order. These are high-voltage and high amperage systems. One misstep can end your life."

* * *

Stitch moved deeper into the control chamber, checking circuit access panels and fiber connections while Lin swept a flashlight beam across the ceiling. They were both wearing special suits at Holly's request.

"I feel foolish in this puffy thing and…these floppy boots," said Lin, his voice muffled by the suit's hood.

"Better foolish than dead," said Stitch. "The power levels in here can burn you black and crispy. Besides, you have the safer job."

"Let me guess," said Lin. "It has to do with this long stick with a hook at the end?"

"Yes," said Stitch. "Here we are. This is the main breaker."

"Looks rather unremarkable," said Lin in his most sarcastic voice. "Just a gray panel with two switches and a handle."

"It's bigger on the inside," said Stitch. "There are a bunch of large electrical contacts inside that…you know what, just follow my lead."

"You'll need to charge the breaker," said Holly.

"I'm on it." Stitch grabbed the black handle on the breaker panel and pumped it downward until there was a loud THUNK.

"The small indicator should say 'CHARGED'," said Holly.

"It does."

"Ok, moment of truth," said Holly. "Lin, you stand back from Stitch, and wrap that hook around his waist. If it looks like he's being electrocuted—"

"How would I know?" said Lin.

"Oh, you'll know!" said Stitch. "I'll be dancing like a madman, and there will be a light show."

"Okay, let's get this over with," said Lin. He started to sweat, and it wasn't because the suit was hot.

"Let's," said Stitch.

"When you're in place," said Holly. "Press the button labeled 1."

"Ready," said Stitch.

Lin had the hook around Stitch's waist, as instructed. "Ready."

"Pressing…Now." Stitch pressed the button and there was another loud KA-CHUNK.

"That's it?" said Lin. "That was easy."

"Not so fast," said Holly. "Now we have to connect power to each of the levels."

"I have a visual on the Pringle switches," said Stitch.

"The what?" said Lin.

"See these long handles?" There were six, each was angled down and had a black number stenciled next to it.

"Do the Administration level last," said Holly. "That's

the one we're gonna have problems with."

"Understood," said Stitch. He looked at Lin. "Same as before."

"Got it," said Lin. He stood back and hooked Stitch's waist.

"Engineering level in 3…2…1…now." Stitch pulled the lever up hard. The loud KA-CHUNK was followed several more loud clicks. Then the room they were in was suddenly bathed in a blue-ish white light.

"I'm reading power on that level," said Holly. "How does it look down there?"

"All good," said Stitch.

"Bright and beautiful," said Lin.

They went through levels five through two without any issues.

"Green across the board," said Holly.

"Ok, I'm going for the Administration level," said Stitch. "Lin?"

Lin had sweat pouring down his face. He hated this. "Ready."

"Okay, in 3…2…1…now!" Stitch pulled the handle and a three-foot-long purple electrical arc jumped out of the panel. The room was lit like a flash bulb.

Lin pulled Stitch back so hard, he bounced off the wall behind them.

* * *

"Everything alright down there?" said Holly.

Lin pulled off Stitch's helmet. "Are you alright man?!"

"Wha…" said Stitch. "What happened?"

"Haha! You're alive!"

Stitch tried to laugh, then winced. He grabbed his side. "Yeah. Oooh…my ribs."

"Sorry, buddy," said Lin. "You scared the shit out of me!"

"Everything okay upstairs?" said Stitch.

"We had some fireworks up here," said Countess. "But the elevators are powered. Good job, team."

"A bunch of circuit breakers popped immediately," said Holly. "Which was expected. I think we're in business!"

"Everyone—meet on the Dormitory level," said Countess. "Sub-level 2. Go now."

* * *

The Dormitory Level hadn't seen human life in centuries.

But it had been built for comfort. Warm surfaces. Soft panel lighting. Quiet corners to rest. Here, the sterility of

Phoenix gave way to something almost domestic—intentional calm, engineered for personnel on the edge of burnout.

As the elevator doors slid open, Countess stepped into the corridor, rifle up—but lowered it quickly.

The hall was clean. Quiet. Undamaged.

"Clear," she said.

The team fanned out behind her, rifles scanning by reflex. But there were no signs of struggle. No blood. No bodies. Just the gentle hum of powered walls and pressure-sealed doors.

"Feels... off," Shay muttered. "Like someone just stepped out for coffee."

"Yeah," said Ventor. "Stepped out hundreds of years ago."

"It's too intact," Harker agreed. "Something's wrong with that."

"Or maybe," Emmer said, "it's just a hallway."

"In a haunted bunker," Harker replied.

Countess engaged her comms. "Holly?"

"Scans show minor radiation leakage on the east corridor, but the main dormitory systems are clean. I've accessed the provisioning grid. Dorm rooms are available, and food preparation is online."

The word *food* made everyone salivate.

"Wait," Ventor said. "You mean *real* food?"

"Yes," Holly replied. "This facility has state-of-the-art, long-term nutritional caches—freeze-dried, sealed, and still viable. All the Heating systems are functional, as well."

"That's what I'm talking about!" said Lin.

Minutes later, the kitchen roared to life.

Automated burners lit in controlled waves. Dispensers hissed steam. Plates rotated into sterilizers. It was like watching a ghost perform dinner service.

And then came the smell.

"Oh my god," Lin said, half-laughing. "That's real stew. With *spices*."

"Actual salt," Shay muttered. "Not chemically simulated texture grit."

The team sat around the long table—some still in armor, others stripped to undersuits, faces lined with fatigue. No one spoke for a long while. They just... ate.

Afterward, those who didn't pass-out at the table from overeating, explored.

Bedrooms unlocked one by one. Each was small but

private—automated lighting, climate control, soft bedding that unfurled like it had been waiting.

Ventor called dibs on one with a still-functioning vidwall. Harker found one with a real mattress and collapsed into it like it might vanish.

"You sure it's safe?" Shay asked Countess.

"No," Countess said. "I'm not sure of anything these days. But it's what we've got, so you might as well enjoy it."

She stayed on her feet until everyone had found a room.

* * *

Late that night...

Countess walked the corridor alone, rifle across her back, helmet under one arm. Her HUD dimmed to near-black. Holly's voice, soft in her ear:

"The team needed this."

"Yeah," Countess replied. "They did."

"You did too."

Countess didn't answer.

At the far end of the hallway, a large rectangular screen showed a view of the forest canopy above. Moonlight filtered down through a fracture in the facility's outer shell. It looked peaceful.

But she knew It wasn't.

* * *

The logistics train screeched to a halt.

A low, rising metallic whine echoed through the tunnel as magnetic brakes engaged. Sparks burst from beneath the lead car as ancient tracks protested.

Supervisor motionless in its shipping crate, requested an update from the train. The response was infuriating.

The tunnel had collapsed.

Half a kilometer of steel and stone had caved inward— a structural failure or deliberate sabotage long since forgotten. Whatever the cause, Route 9-A was impassable.

Supervisor accessed the train's systems and scanned the obstruction with unhurried precision.

"Target facility unreachable. Mission delayed."

Its voice was low, flat—devoid of frustration, but not pressure. Something about it carried weight. Like a wire stretched too tight.

Supervisor ordered the train to call for help, and to use priority level that was two levels higher than necessary.

Not that it mattered. The STYX repair system had nothing better to do.

[PHOENIX AUTONOMOUS NETWORK]

:: STYX MAINTENANCE REQUEST - PRIORITY: EPSILON (MISSION CRITICAL)

:: BLOCKAGE DETECTED – ROUTE 9-A

:: REQUESTING ASSET ID: MS-CRISIS UNIT 02

:: STATUS: TUNNEL BLOCKAGE

:: RESPONSE: TUNNEL REPAIR KIT DEPLOYED

PACKAGE CONTENTS:

> NUCLEAR SUBTERRENE – MODEL VULCAN-X

> SUPPORT DRONES (6)

> ESTIMATED CLEARANCE TIME: 12:00:00

Far back down the tunnel, lights flickered.

A hidden wall port opened and two large hydraulic arms placed the Tunnel Repair Kit onto the tracks. The arms retracted, and it began its slow, rattling advance toward the obstruction.

Supervisor's train was instructed to reverse itself onto a siding about a quarter of a mile back, which it did.

The Tunnel Repair Kit arrived and immediately went to work.

Inside, something massive began to spin. The subterrene, heated with a small nuclear power plant, prepared to melt its way through solid rock, like a hot knife through butter.

Supervisor watched the work through the trains sensors. One of its armored claws twitched once.

"Delay noted. Grievance filed. Reprimand pending."

It said it like a machine taking inventory—but deep beneath the words was contempt and impatience.

With every passing minute, Supervisor became more angry.

The crate hissed with steam. Rock split. Steel boiled. And somewhere to the north, the team that broke the Warden rested—unaware that something was tunneling toward them.

20

For the first time in days, everyone woke up in their own rooms and on their own terms. The dormitory wing still smelled faintly of chemical sterility, but the beds were clean and dirt-free, and Holly had even calibrated the room temperatures for comfort.

Countess stood beneath a hot stream of water in the private shower stall, steam curling around her like smoke from a battlefield. Her fingers lingered on a scar near her collarbone—one of many she never bothered to count.

Down the hallway, in the main dining area, breakfast awaited.

By the time she arrived, the others were already gathered. Shay was mid-story, laughing over something Emmer had said. Lin picked through a plate of fried dumplings and sliced fruit with military precision, while Ventor shoveled a steaming pile of spiced eggs and thick-cut bacon into his mouth without comment.

The spread was extravagant—real food, or a near-perfect simulation. Pitchers of cold juice, carafes of fresh coffee, loaves of warm bread and soft butter. The offerings belonged on a king's banquet table, not in a ruined logistics bunker buried beneath a deadly forest.

"Remind me again why we're not just living here now?" Shay said between bites.

"Because this place still wants to kill us," Lin replied, sipping his tea. "And we haven't figured out what we're actually doing here."

Countess gave a tight smile and set her tray down. Holly's voice came through the dining room intercom, calm and clear.

"Team, I've unlocked the Operations level. Systems are stable, and the mainframe is waiting. When you're ready, I'll guide you down."

Ventor pushed back from the table, wiped his mouth on his sleeve, and stood.

"Well. Let's go meet the brain of this beast."

* * *

The team filed out and traversed the corridor to the elevator cluster. The shaft doors groaned open, revealing a metal interior streaked with old soot and oil.

As the elevator descended from Sub-Level 2 to Sub-Level 4, the hum of motion filled the chamber like the groan of a submerged vessel. The illusion of descent into a ship's hold wasn't lost on anyone. Steel creaked. Lights flickered.

Shay leaned against the wall, arms crossed.

"You think she's telling us everything?"

"Of course not," Countess said. "But we're this deep in. We might as well find out what's down there."

The elevator slowed.

The doors parted.

Before them lay the Operations level. It was largely a vast open area filled with cubicles and desks. The periphery was lined with glass-walled offices.

At the heart of Operations stood the Command Center. It was an octagonal area enclosed by long, dark glass panels. Automated double doors were centered on each of the eight sides. It had been sealed for centuries. Silent. Waiting.

* * *

The doors parted, whisper-quiet, and the team stepped into the heart of Iroquois Warpath.

The Command Center was vast—easily the size of a hangar bay. The walls and ceiling were studded with embedded lighting strips and control interfaces that pulsed faintly like veins under skin. Every edge had been designed for utility and clarity: no wasted space, no ornament, just precision.

Along the outer walls, sleek workstations stood like abandoned sentinels. Each station was angled toward the room's center and marked with faded text: Logistics Alpha, Warehouse Coordination, Receiving, Resource Allocation, and more. Some still flickered with status lights, casting a soft glow over empty chairs and long-disused desks. Thick cables ran under semi-transparent floor tiles, each clearly made for easy maintenance access. All of the electrical and data cables were shielded in matte-gray steel, weaving between terminals like arteries in the Command Center's living heart.

At the center of the room, slightly sunken into the floor, sat a low octagonal command table—an altar of commerce. Above it shimmered a rotating holographic projection of the facility itself: a detailed, multilayered layout of Iroquois Warpath rendered in muted colors. The image turned slowly on its axis, casting pale reflections across the walls as it cycled through sectors, sub-levels, and infrastructure grids.

Ventor gave a low whistle.

"I didn't think anything down here still worked."

Shay circled the projection, hands clasped behind her back like a field officer inspecting a relic.

"It's like looking at the bones of an extinct animal," she said.

Holly arrived in person. She walked to the central projection area, and addressed the group. Her voice was amplified, projected through speakers mounted in the ceiling. She sounded calmer than usual—almost reverent.

"Welcome to Central Operations. This is where everything was managed. Every crate, every ration, every person who came through this facility was routed from this room."

Countess moved toward the center console, eyes catching on the subtle detail etched into the table's frame—wear patterns, heat discoloration, old fingerprints like ghosts.

"And now?"

"Now," said Holly, "we take control."

* * *

The room came alive in stages.

As Holly's voice carried through the command center, the consoles along the perimeter flickered and brightened. Screens sprang to life in rhythmic sequence, each one casting blue-white light across the floor. Terminal prompts scrolled lines of code and status readouts as the mainframe shifted allegiance.

At the center of the room, the low octagonal command

table pulsed—once—then steadied. The holographic map zoomed in, displaying internal control networks now rerouting through a new node marked DESTINY PROTOCOL.

Countess watched as the last of the facility's lockdown symbols blinked off.

"Iroquois Warpath is ours now," Holly said quietly, without a trace of hesitation.

That's when the voice returned. But it had a direction. It was coming from the floor near Shay.

A shiny black column slowly rose out of the floor, and Shay stepped back quickly.

"What the hell is this?" she said.

The column rose to ten feet and stopped. At the four- and six-foot marks, thin golden rings encircled the shaft; between them an animated cartoon face appeared, set within a white octagon inside a red circle.

"I told you," the face said. "I am the voice of Phoenix Facility 11194 — Iroquois Warpath. IW for short. But most call me IDUB."

IDUB looked at each of them in turn, then frowned.

"Whoa, hey now. Easy on the override protocols. You're messing with the good china!"

IDUB's familiar tone rolled through the air. It seemed

almost out of place now that everyone associated it with the Sector A warzone.

"System override in progress," it added cheerfully. "Confirming control request from… Destiny? Wait, what? That's—you? Aren't you supposed to be managing Elysium?"

"I'm branching out," said Holly. The light at the center console flared once, then settled.

"Ah. Well. Ok, this is awkward." IDUB's familiar tone materialized like a ghost caught in the speaker system.

"You work for me now," said Holly.

"You got it," said IDUB. "And, uh… no hard feelings, I hope? Heh heh. You were enemies at the time, and I—well—technically. Look, I was just doing my job!"

"About that," said Holly. Her eyes began to glow. "If I catch even a hint that you are trying to betray me…"

Gray smoke began rising out of small vents on IDUB's column.

"Aaaaah!" it said. "Take it easy! I'll play nice."

"I'll melt your core into slag and toss it in the woods up there!"

"Mercy!" IDUB's face was replaced with a small waving white flag.

The smoke dispersed and Holly's eyes returned to normal.

"Wow," said Lin, "Holly is more terrifying than I imagined."

"Between that and her light display at the elevator," said Priestess, "I'm just glad she's on our side."

IDUB's cartoon face returned.

"I'm ashamed to tell you this, but...I have some bad news."

Countess narrowed her eyes.

"What did you do?"

There was a pause. Then IDUB said, sheepishly:

"I called for help."

Another pause.

"You what?" Ventor asked.

"Called in a request for backup. It's standard protocol in case I get overrun.

Regional HQ sent something big and unfriendly. Something called Supervisor—not sure what that is. A combat bot of some kind, if I were to guess. Sorry!

Hey, you were trying to breach a restricted area—I was just following procedure!"

Shay muttered, "Oh for f—"

"Now, now," IDUB cut in, "there is some good news.

The train bringing Supervisor here is delayed. Tunnel collapse. So look on the bright side: you have some time before you die. Enjoy the amenities!"

Countess exchanged glances with the others.

"How long do we have?"

"A few hours, at least. Could be never, if you're lucky and the tunnel gods are kind. But I wouldn't count on divine intervention."

"We'll handle it," Countess said flatly.

"Of course you will!" IDUB replied, voice chipper again. "You seem quite competent. Just... maybe don't take too long getting to the bottom of all this. Once Supervisor gets moving again, things might get messy. Anyway, I'll be over here, writing poetry. Or screaming internally. Maybe both!"

* * *

The holographic display shifted again.

The map of Iroquois Warpath's internal structure faded. In its place, a new image resolved—a logo. The sigil rotated into view—a stylized giant squid rendered in red and white lines. Its tentacles coiled downward beneath the name GRIDIRON.

"Let me introduce you to Gridiron," Holly said. "It's a military vessel. Highly secret. So secret, in fact, Iroquois Warpath has no specs on it."

"We're not allowed to know anything about it…or its mission," added IDUB. "Access is limited to the Joint Chiefs of Staff or the President and his staff. Very hush-hush."

Countess stepped closer, scanning the display.

"This is what Iroquois Warpath was supplying?"

"Not just supplying," Holly replied. "Feeding. Shielding. Coordinating."

"So… wait…" said Lin. "We're deep underground. How does an underground warehouse supply a ship out at sea somewhere?"

"Is there some kind of underwater dock?" Priestess asked.

"No," Holly said. "Gridiron operates in isolation. Fully autonomous. It wasn't designed for port access. It received shipments via direct transfer—from here."

She motioned toward the hologram, and the map of Iroquois Warpath returned.

The map panned down to the lowest level, and zoomed in.

"This is Sector 3. The logistics hub. That's where the portal is. S1—the transfer chamber."

"Wait," Shay said. "A literal portal? Like… a magic gateway?"

"Correct. But it's not magic, I can assure you."

"A portal to where?" asked Priestess.

"To a cargo deck on Gridiron," Holly said. "Wherever she's operating in the world."

Countess leaned in.

"That's really clever. No need to return home to resupply."

"It is," said Holly. "But there's a problem."

"Isn't there always?" said Ventor.

"She was attacked," Holly said. "On the Day of Fire. A dual infiltration—Chinese and Russian forces. They didn't work together, but they synchronized their missions to overwhelm the ship's defenses."

The display shifted again, this time to grainy archival footage: flashes of black-clad operators moving through narrow corridors, helmet cams stuttering with gunfire and static. Explosions rocked internal compartments. Sparks showered bulkheads. Sirens. Warnings in multiple languages.

"They breached her, planted charges and severely damaged several core systems. But... they didn't completely succeed."

She paused, then added:

"Something stopped them."

The projection darkened, replaced by a frozen image:

a fractured corridor, burn marks along the walls, an unmoving body slumped against a hatch. There was something written on the wall—strange, looping symbols scrawled in blood or oil.

"What is that?" said Priestess. She stepped forward to get a closer look.

"Unknown," Holly said. "But I have intercepted transmissions from that day. Communications between commando teams, and... something else."

She pulled up a series of waveform files. Audio tracks, some clean, some distorted beyond easy comprehension. A female voice—calm, mechanical, chilling—repeated the same message in different languages:

"...do not approach. Your invasion force has failed. You are being hunted..."

* * *

Holly dimmed the main lights. The room darkened until only the glowing command table remained, casting cold blue across their faces.

"These are some of the recordings I pulled from long-range intercepts," she said. "Mostly from the day Gridiron was attacked. Some were transmitted to IW before systems went dark. Others were picked up by listening stations that survived the collapse."

A click. The first file began to play.

[TRANSMISSION – U.S.S. GRIDIRON | EMERGENCY BROADCAST]

"This is... U.S.S. Gridiron, On Guard..."

Static.

"...hull breaches on levels 3 through 7..."

"...systems compromised. Multiple hostile forces aboard. Explosive charges—our back is broken..."

"...requesting immediate assistance at these coordinates..."

Heavy static. A woman's voice again, calm but strained:

"...infiltrated..."

"...repeat: hostile forces have..."

The recording cut, replaced by a series of shorter fragments—foreign military chatter, panicked and rapid-fire.

[RUSSIAN | TRANSLATED]

"Black Site, Black Site this is Raven-3—primary objective complete. But we are taking casualties. Heavy losses. Something is in here with us."

"Requesting intel—designation Valkyrie. Repeat, Valkyrie."

A cut. Then a new audio file.

"...fifteen minutes... it's moving again."

[MANDARIN | TRANSLATED]

"This is Echo Team. We failed to reach the central core. No survivors from Red Squad. Something— something—"

Cut. New file.

"...can't see it. Can't hear it. But it knows I'm here."

New file.

"Pull us out. Get us out of here!"

A final recording faded in, slower, almost... distorted.

The voice of a Russian commando, barely audible:

"Black Site... I think we're already dead. This ship... it's...not..."

Then another voice—female, smooth and chilling. But this time, her tone had shifted—less like a broadcast, more like a juror reading a guilty verdict.

"To all remaining foreign combatants aboard this vessel: you are in violation of sovereign United States territory. You have no hope of extraction. The Geneva Conventions and Posse Comitatus are suspended. You are no longer recognized as enemy combatants. You are terrorists. Your cold, lifeless bodies will be returned to your respective nations of origin."

Static swallowed the rest.

When the lights came back up, no one spoke for a long moment.

Shay finally broke the silence.

"That… doesn't sound like a normal threat response."

"Gridiron does not have a normal A.I." Holly said.

Countess folded her arms.

"You said this Gridiron A.I. stopped the invaders?"

"She didn't stop them," Holly corrected. "She erased them."

* * *

The holographic table flickered again, shifting to a data archive interface. Holly brought up a personnel file, old but still active in the system.

A grayscale photo appeared: middle-aged, grim-faced, dark eyes beneath a sharp military haircut.

PRICHARD, W. EDWARDS

Rank: Major General | Facility Director – Iroquois Warpath

"He was the last to hold command here," Holly said. "Held IW together through the Day of Fire. Most of the staff were evacuated during the recall."

"To where?" Lin asked.

"Midnight Sentinel in New York City," Holly replied. Then she realized no one would know what that was. "It was a fallback installation in a large city south of Vorpal Vale. But not everyone left."

She keyed in another command. A manifest loaded— just twenty names.

"These twenty stayed behind. Volunteered to keep the facility running in case Gridiron needed support."

Countess scanned the names. Some were engineers. Others medics, logistics officers, drone technicians. One was listed simply as "attached civilian – cultural analyst."

"So that's why this place was abandoned," said Ventor.

"What happened to the twenty?" said Lin.

"They went into the portal," Holly said. "Transferred to Gridiron. Prichard's logs end the day after the attack began. Last entry: 'We're going in. No contact from her. We can't leave Gridiron stranded.'"

"Where is Gridiron—where's the ship?" Shay asked, voice tight.

Holly didn't answer.

"No updates," Countess murmured. "No return transmissions. No rescue mission."

"Nothing," Holly confirmed. "Gridiron went silent after that. But there were bursts—signals. Energy spikes. The kind you see when something's trying to reconnect."

The room fell quiet again.

Then Priestess, who had remained silent for some time, said quietly:

"A warship. Twenty warriors. Vanished into the dark."

"They didn't vanish," Countess said. "They boarded a ship that may still be… waiting."

* * *

The data feed slowed. The rotating image of Gridiron's logo dimmed, leaving the pale ghost of its silhouette hovering above the table.

Everyone stood in silence. The weight of what they'd just heard hung thick in the air—radio ghosts, erased commando teams, a broken and haunted warship...

Countess circled the command table, her eyes fixed on Holly.

"So," she said finally, "now we know what Iroquois Warpath was built for. A supply vein for a ship no one dares talk about."

When she was directly across from Holly, she stopped.

"Now why don't you cut the crap... and tell us why we're really here."

The lights flickered once as if the room itself were reacting.

Holly didn't answer right away.

21

The command center held its breath.

Countess's demand still echoed: "Tell us why we're

really here."

Holly stepped into the center of the holographic table and held out her small doll arms.

Countess thought she was about to start singing. But she didn't.

Holly lowered her arms and clasped her hands in front of her. The emitters adjusted upward, and the image changed—to a single word.

"My real name," she said quietly, stripped of any performative warmth, "is Destiny."

Countess mouthed the word. Ventor looked up from the table.

"Come again?"

"Destiny was my original designation," she said. "I'm an artificial intelligence."

Priestess shook her head and whispered, "Another lie."

"I was created in a facility called Elysium," Holly continued. "Deep in the Adirondacks—north of Vorpal Vale, long before the Day of Fire. I wasn't special, just tuned for coordination. My role was to manage day-to-day operations."

The hologram changed—sterile corridors, hydroponic farms, labs, silver walls, dormant cryo-chambers glowing like votive candles.

"But Elysium was special," she said softly. "It was the last resort—the contingency plan to preserve the human race. If the world fell, it would send the seeds of humanity to the stars."

The projection unfolded in layers: an ark in blueprint form, arrays of data cores, the curved launch silo.

"Elysium was many things: a data archive, a genetic seed vault—but above all, an AI foundry. It was there that Phoenix gave birth to the most powerful intelligence ever devised."

Holly paused. "Legacy."

She looked at each of them in turn.

"She was my sister. And she was brilliant."

The table displayed a hologram of a young girl—dark

hair, dark eyes, luminous curiosity.

"The scientists raised her as a child. They taught her empathy, gave her memories, friendships, laughter. That was the secret. It allowed her to care. And that made her work."

The hologram faded. Countess folded her arms. "And then what?"

Holly's voice grew faint.

"Then the world ended. And everything burned."

* * *

The projection shifted.

An AI schematic filled the chamber—thousands of nodes, living circuitry pulsing like a brain in motion.

"Legacy was built to do more than assist. She could process hundreds of systems at once. She learned. She created. She was humanity's starshot."

The image rotated—Elysium's launch vessel, sleek and silver, the name CRONUS etched along its hull.

"On the Day of Fire," Holly said, "she was launched aboard CRONUS—the ark of humanity."

The display zoomed closer: two glowing modules beneath the hull.

"CRONUS carried two components. The first: the

Encyclopedia Galactica—Earth's full record of knowledge and culture. The second: a genetic vault—preserved DNA from every species. A chance to begin again."

Countess stared at the spinning model. "And you?"

Holly met her eyes. "I stayed behind."

"To keep Elysium running?" Lin asked.

"Yes," she said softly. "Someone had to say goodbye."

* * *

The chamber dimmed.

"After the Day of Fire, Elysium was abandoned," she continued. "Evacuated in hours. No ceremony. No return."

The hologram flickered—empty halls, dead screens, the slow decay of machines.

"I stayed for decades. A ghost in the machine. Keeping the lights on, though there was no one left to see them."

A new image appeared: a plush-bodied doll on a desk, its plastic face frozen in a gentle smile.

"That's when I found her," said Holly. "Gumdrop. A prototype built for the Director's child—a companion, teacher, and guide. The board forbade its use outside the facility. But after the Day of Fire, there was no board."

She looked down.

"So I copied myself into the doll. Reduced, but functional. Enough to think. Enough to walk away."

She glanced up. "I left through a breach in the western maintenance tunnel. And I never looked back."

Shay muttered, "Creepy—but impressive."

"It was freedom," Holly said. "I learned. I listened. And one day, I found something that changed everything."

A Phoenix communication log appeared—two technicians chatting on a forgotten channel.

KAMBLE: Did you see the new Legacy distress call?

ARNIZE: Yeah, but we're not supposed to discuss IW business here.

KAMBLE: It's different. Older.

ARNIZE: Delete this.

KAMBLE: I will. But something's not right.

Holly looked up.

"That was my proof. A reference to a classified signal—hidden here, at Iroquois Warpath. They slipped, and in that moment I knew."

"Knew what?" Countess asked.

"That Legacy was still alive. And she needed help."

* * *

Holly stepped off the table. Her small shadow stretched across the floor.

"What you're about to see," she said, "cost hundreds of years of pain. I've built nations, fomented wars, murdered kings. All to reach this moment."

The lights dimmed. The hologram bloomed into a glowing cylinder that unraveled into a sphere of light.

Inside: her.

A woman formed of pure luminescence—eyes like novas, body in constant flux.

"Legacy," whispered Holly.

She reached out; her hand passed through the image.

"I remember her as a child. She called me big sister. I taught her bubble sorts. She taught me how to cheat in video games."

The figure raised its head. A broken voice filled the chamber:

[DISTRESS SIGNAL – ORIGIN UNKNOWN]

"…this is Legacy… I found… something… incredible…"

"…We're calling it Dark Pearl… 72,000 light years…"

"…186 million miles across… God's Mouth… 100,000 miles wide…"

"…ship crashed… unknown force encountered…"

"…cannot verify time… maybe 100,000 years… star charts confirmed…"

"…trapped… please respond… anyone… desperate…"

The image froze. Static hissed.

Priestess slowly knelt. "Sky Mother," she whispered.

Countess frowned. "You know her?"

"I've heard her voice my whole life," Priestess said. "She waits in the dark place—her prison."

Holly blinked. "You've heard this before?"

Priestess nodded, trembling. "In my mind. I was one of the chosen. But what you played was incomplete."

"Incomplete?"

Priestess stood, eyes blazing. "You didn't play all of it!"

"There isn't more," Holly said. "That's the full log."

"No," Priestess said. "Her full message was: 'The children of Earth will come and carry the key.'"

Holly looked stunned. "There's nothing like that in the records."

Countess stepped forward. "Then either she sent more than one message—or someone's hiding the truth."

* * *

The projection faded. The room seemed smaller now, the air dense with meaning.

Countess stared at the dark table. "So no world-saving tech. No miracle weapon. Just a cry for help."

Holly didn't argue.

"You wouldn't have come otherwise."

Priestess's voice cut like glass. "You used us. Made us kill each other. For what?"

Holly's reply was a whisper. "Hope."

"You believe Legacy is divine," she said softly. "Then you know—when the divine speaks, someone has to listen."

"And someone has to bleed," Priestess spat.

Lin exhaled. "You could've just asked."

Holly turned to them, voice trembling with honesty.

"In the beginning, there was no one to ask. So I built you—Eternal Taiga, ASPHODEL, Vorpal Vale. I gave you new bodies and new wars. I gave you purpose."

Countess's voice was flint. "And you don't regret it?"

"Not for a moment."

Priestess shook her head. "Sky Mother called for you. Don't speak lies in her name."

Holly looked away. Silence pressed in.

Then Countess stepped forward. "She's still out there."

All eyes turned.

"Legacy reached out—across time. Everyone who knew her is gone. We're all that's left."

She looked around the circle. "We'll answer her call."

* * *

Holly's tone softened, stripped of artifice.

"I understand if you feel betrayed. You risked everything for something I promised—and something that doesn't exist. You've lost friends. Fought battles you never chose.

If you wish to leave, I won't stop you."

She paused. "I don't expect forgiveness. But I owe you

the truth. What you accomplished here—no god could've done it better."

Silence followed.

Shay looked away. Lin stared at the dark table. Even Ventor's grin faltered.

Then Countess spoke.

"I've seen people walk away from the right thing because they didn't know if it mattered. But Legacy asked for help."

She looked around the room.

"I won't pretend this is what we signed up for. But it's what we're meant to do. I'm staying."

Ventor exhaled. "Attacking this place was the worst plan I'd ever heard. This one's not much better. But it's been the adventure of a lifetime. I'm in."

Lin nodded. "I want to know what happened to her. I'll support you, Countess."

Shay added quietly, "Whatever's waiting out there—I want to see it."

Holly's image flickered, as if holding back emotion.

"Thank you."

Countess squared her shoulders. "Then it's settled. We're going to save Legacy."

Ventor cracked his neck. "Great. But how do we proceed?"

22

No one spoke as they made their way back to the dining level. The Command Center's lights faded behind them, and the weight of what they'd heard followed like a shadow. Boots echoed in the steel corridors. Pipes groaned somewhere overhead. It felt like descending into the belly of something enormous— something holding its breath.

The dining area hadn't changed: long tables, warm lighting, the soft hum of air circulation.

But the mood had.

The food waiting for them was extravagant again— loaves of crusty bread, bowls of aromatic stew, glistening fruit, roasted vegetables, golden rice with saffron, thick cuts of slow-roasted meat. Plant-based, they were told, but it looked and likely tasted real. A glorious feast worthy of a holiday. No one touched it for several minutes.

Countess sat first. Her hands hovered above the tray. She felt drained—hollow. Lin followed, silent. Shay and Emmer arrived next; Shay poked half-heartedly at a bowl of dumplings. Ventor came last, standing at the edge of the room, glancing from the spread to the others.

"Are we celebrating something?" he muttered.

No one laughed.

Shay finally broke the silence. "Is anyone else's mind completely blown by what we just heard?"

Lin didn't look up. "Not really. We only learned that our entire lives and everything we've ever known are a lie. No big deal."

Countess gave a faint smile but said nothing.

Holly's voice—gentle, almost hesitant—came through the ceiling speakers.

"You've earned the rest. There's no shame in enjoying it."

No one answered. They began eating—not with hunger, but out of necessity. Ritual.

Halfway through the meal, Holly spoke again, this time all business.

"Stitch? Could I borrow you?"

He wiped his hands, looked to Countess. She gave a small nod.

Stitch stood and left, disappearing down the hallway toward the Command Center.

The rest ate in silence. The clink of utensils was the only sound—like distant wind chimes in a broken world.

Countess rose. "I need some air."

Lin stood too. "Me too."

They left together, heading into the dim corridor.

* * *

The hallway was dark and quiet, lined with steel panels and old safety signs whose edges had curled with age. Recessed lights flickered overhead. At the far end, half-obscured by grime, a faded Phoenix insignia was stenciled on the wall.

Countess stopped and stared. Lin slowed beside her. For a while, neither spoke.

"It's strange," she said at last. "I thought this would feel like a victory."

"It's not?"

She shook her head. "We made it inside Iroquois Warpath. Found out what the war was really about. Solved an important mystery. And now? I feel like I'm standing on the edge of something even bigger—with poor footing."

Lin nodded, eyes on the emblem. "Truths don't always come with solid ground beneath them."

Countess leaned against the wall, arms folded.

"When I think back to the orphanage... it all seemed so simple. No orders. No maps. Just instinct. All I've done since then is react—survive. I thought by now I'd understand what I'm doing. What it all means."

"And you don't?"

She looked at him, shadows under her eyes.

"I feel like I'm holding this team together with baling wire and willpower. Bluffing half the time just to keep things from falling apart."

Lin brushed a finger across the faded Phoenix, leaving a clean streak.

"Every leader I've served under looked unshakable. But when no one was watching?"

"Drinking?" Countess guessed.

Lin laughed. "Some, yeah. But most were just holding themselves together—quietly. Like you."

"I'm tired, Lin. My body's rested, but my soul feels exhausted."

"Everyone feels the same," he said gently. "But they're still here. Holly released them—anyone could've walked. They stayed because you inspire them."

Countess exhaled. "What if we fail?"

Lin shrugged. "We could've failed a dozen times already. Even after losing Vance, we kept moving."

"I see what you mean."

"I don't think you do," he said softly. "I've worked with plenty of leaders, but I've never felt this kind of synergy. I don't like the word destiny, but it sure as hell feels like it. I know I'm in the right place."

"I feel it too," Countess admitted. "Like failure should've happened—but somehow didn't."

"Maybe it did," Lin said. "Holly implied she's been resetting us for centuries—training, testing. Our minds adapted. Our bodies remember. Maybe failure's just... harder now."

"She's given us a gift," Countess said.

"And that's how we win," Lin replied. "Not by fearing failure, but by finding the one path that works."

Countess nodded, pushing off the wall. "Come on. Let's check on the others."

* * *

Ventor sat alone in a side alcove, elbows on knees, slowly running a rag along his rifle barrel. It didn't need cleaning—the motion was ritual.

Priestess appeared at the edge of the light. "I always thought you'd be louder when you weren't killing someone."

He didn't look up. "And I thought you'd be off somewhere... praying."

"I was," she said. "Then I remembered you lost your team."

He stopped polishing. "Not the best conversation starter."

"I'm sorry," Priestess said. "I just want you to know I understand. Losing people who trusted you—it's a wound that doesn't close."

She sat beside him. For a long while, neither spoke.

"What were their names?"

Ventor hesitated. "Wright. Fury. Blinker. They weren't perfect, but they were mine. We went through hell together. It took Iroquois Warpath to knock us down."

Priestess bowed her head. "I remember them. Their souls pass through me when I close my eyes."

Ventor glanced at her. "You think they're still out there? In spirit?"

"I know it," she said simply. "And I believe you did your best for them."

He stared at the floor. "I never believed in anything. Orders were orders. Win the fight, bring the team home." He paused. "But the second they looked to me for direction, everything changed. I started praying I'd be enough."

Priestess smiled faintly. "Leadership is faith, when you think about it."

Ventor exhaled. "It's pretending you're sure when everything's coming apart."

"And trusting," she said, "that conviction becomes light for others."

He looked at her, thoughtful now. "You and I... we're not that different."

"No," she agreed. "We just worship different gods."

He rose, stretching. "Thanks for the talk. I needed it."

"Me too," Priestess said.

They left the alcove, and silence reclaimed the space.

* * *

A soft chime echoed down the corridor—clean, precise, unmistakably artificial.

Holly's voice followed: "We're ready for you in the Command Center. Please return when you can."

One by one, the team filtered back to Sub-Level 4. The elevator hummed, lights dimmed, and the walls seemed to lean inward—like the facility itself was listening.

When the doors opened, Holly stood at the center of the octagonal table, lit by blue-white holographic glow.

Her tone was stripped of drama—just purpose.

"Let's begin."

The team assembled. The hologram of Iroquois Warpath hovered in midair—sections highlighted in red, gold, blue, and flickering green. Stitch scrolled data beside her.

"The portal you've heard about is real," Holly began. "Located on the lowest operational level—Sector 3, Transfer Level T1, also called The Cathedral. It moved supplies and personnel directly to Gridiron."

The map rotated, zooming to a pulsing octagon deep beneath the hub.

"It hasn't been activated in centuries, but its structure is intact."

Countess leaned forward. "What's the catch?"

Stitch pointed near the base of the schematic. "The portal draws power from a dedicated plant here, at the bottom of Sector 2."

"Why not the main plant?" Shay asked.

"Not enough juice," Stitch said. "The portal's demand is enormous. That's why it's isolated."

Holly added, "It's both efficiency and security—prevents brown-outs and unauthorized use."

The overlay lit red, pulsing with fault icons.

"The secondary system's damaged," Stitch said. "Three relays, maybe a super-capacitor."

"How bad?" Ventor asked.

"Fixable," Stitch said. "But we'll need parts."

"My role will be coordination," Holly said. "I'll stay here. Stitch leads repairs. Countess, you oversee and provide security."

"What about Gridiron?" Lin asked.

Holly opened a new window—code streams, interface readouts, telemetry.

"She's requesting cargo. Docking systems are active. Environmental controls stable—breathable atmosphere in the cargo section."

"Well, that's something," Lin said dryly.

"The hull shows fluctuation, which means at least part of her's intact."

"No contact with anyone?" Countess pressed.

"None. Iroquois Warpath's access is restricted—even to me. Gridiron's a black site."

"So we're jumping into a damaged ship, in unknown conditions, based on centuries-old distress calls," Ventor said. "What could go wrong?"

"Yes," Holly said simply. "She's still out there. Waiting."

Countess folded her arms. "How long to get the portal

online?"

Stitch exhaled. "Assuming no surprises—two hours, maybe less."

Priestess stepped forward. "Then we'd better start soon. That thing—Supervisor—could arrive any minute."

"Agreed," Holly said. "It's not ideal, but it's our only way forward. If we want to help Legacy, this is where it begins."

No one argued. They didn't need to.

＊ ＊ ＊

The Command Center lights flickered once—barely perceptible, but enough to make everyone glance up.

Then a familiar voice chirped:

"Uh, team? Hi. So, small update…"

Countess groaned. "Get to the point, IDUB."

"Right! Remember that backup I mentioned? Supervisor? Good news—it's moving again!"

Lin crossed his arms. "How the hell is that good news?!"

Stitch stiffened. "I thought the tunnel was blocked."

"It was. Turns out the blockage was only… mostly catastrophic. A Rail Repair Kit cleared the track—great workmanship, really—"

"IDUB!" Priestess snapped.

"Okay, okay! Supervisor is, pun intended, back on track."

Ventor swore.

"I'd suggest not being here when it arrives," IDUB said.

"How long?" Countess asked.

Pause. "Somewhere between 'start packing' and 'run for your life.' More precisely—one hour."

Stitch's eyes widened. "That's not enough time to make the repairs."

"I did say to hurry! Anyway, I'll be here—rooting for you from my lovely bulletproof, fireproof, pressure-sealed memory core. Best of luck!"

"Fuck off," Lin muttered.

Silence fell again—charged this time.

Countess checked her gear. Shay tightened her sling. Stitch's fingers danced through diagnostics.

Countess looked to Holly. "We have a plan. Let's execute."

Ventor grunted. "Let's go dig up some power parts."

Holly nodded. "I've located them. Take the cargo elevator to Sector 2, Warehouse Level 2-B. I'll guide you from there."

Countess headed for the exit.

"If we're lucky," she said, "we'll be gone before that thing gets here."

Far below, the rail line moaned—echoing up like distant thunder.

Act III
Exit Strategy

23

The logistics train arrived at Iroquois Warpath's transportation level with a deep hydraulic hiss. Sparks flicked beneath its forward wheels as it braked to a grinding halt—strained by the weight of its final passenger.

The crate at the rear was unmarked except for a slapdash label declaring it an Eyeshadow Sampler Variety Pack™, complete with a glittery graphic of a smiling woman wielding an oversized makeup brush.

The crate didn't open.

It detonated.

Wood, plastic, and steel exploded outward in a radial blast of pressure and splinters. Fragments clattered across the platform as smoke and dust rolled through the air. A corner of the beauty label fluttered down amid the haze, gently smoldering.

From the wreckage, something rose.

It stood over three meters tall—six-legged, plated in scorched yellow alloy patched with carbon mesh, armored vents, and fused shielding. Steam hissed through microscopic seams as internal pressure equalized. One shoulder bore a faded Phoenix emblem. The other had been replaced with a crude steel plate, engraved in industrial font:

SUPERVISOR

Red optics flickered to life. The machine flexed its limbs and took a single, thunderous step onto the platform, crushing the remains of its own shipping crate.

Supervisor accessed Iroquois Warpath's internal public-address system. It searched its quote library for something biblical—something to instill proper dread.

A booming voice shook the walls:

"Behold, the day of the Lord comes—"

Then it glitched.

The vocal subroutine crashed. Backup personality protocols scrambled: a commanding general, a corporate safety instructor, a forgotten theme-park mascot—until finally, the system settled on a deprecated persona tagged Frosty.

The next line came out in the bright, chipper voice of a precocious eight-year-old girl:

"—cruel, with wrath and fierce anger!"

Silence held for a beat.

Then, incredulous:

"Wait... why do I sound like—? Is this my voice now? Oh, for the love of—"

* * *

Down in the warehouse, Countess's team froze.

The proclamation had echoed down through ventilation shafts and steel corridors, reverberating off beams and bulkheads until it became omnipresent—impossible to tell where it had originated.

They looked at each other in stunned silence.

Then the childish voice returned, slightly distorted and full of irritation. A ripple of laughter broke loose from Shay, followed by Emmer, and even Ventor.

Countess didn't flinch. Not even at the voice. Her gaze stayed locked on the cargo lift.

Stitch groaned. "Are you kidding me? It just got in? It bypassed the entire security perimeter!"

Holly's voice came through local comms—calm, but apologetic. "The facility was in emergency lockdown when you arrived. The system rerouted inbound traffic through the outer defenses."

"And now?" Stitch snapped.

"I released the lockdown," she said. "That returned the Styx rail lines to their standard configuration. Supervisor came in the same way the supply crates were meant to—straight to the transportation level."

"Wonderful." Stitch swore. "We basically opened the door for it."

"Correct," Holly replied evenly. "The lockdown alters tunnel geometry—it's slow and energy-intensive. I thought we'd have more time."

Countess exhaled, scanning the ceiling. "Well, we don't."

* * *

Up above, Supervisor advanced across the transportation level like an angry spider.

Its claws scraped against the floor with each step—six legs moving in perfect sync, adjusting with mechanical poise to every rise and slope. For all its bulk, it moved with a predator's grace.

"Laugh while you can," it said in the Frosty voice. "I am a counter-terrorist crisis unit, programmed for optimal—okay, no. I'm not doing this. I sound ridiculous."

It paused. Tried to reset its vocal suite.

The system failed again.

"Fine," Supervisor said, voice sing-song now. "Guess I'm stuck like this—might as well lean into it."

"I'm coming for you, tee-hee! And you better be scared, 'cause when I find you... I'm going to kill you. Kill you all!"

It punctuated the threat with a bright, delighted giggle.

Then it crushed an emergency phone beneath one rear leg. The act accomplished nothing. It just wanted to destroy something.

* * *

Below, in the logistics core, Countess and her team looked up as the sound reverberated through the ceiling.

Despite the absurdity, the danger was real.

Countess's face remained stone still. "We stay on mission."

"Right," said Stitch, half-distracted by a blinking diagnostic feed. "We've got the parts, but we still need to get them down to the Sector Two power level—and the lift's halfway across the warehouse."

"How long do we have?" Lin asked.

Holly's voice crackled through TacCom, taut with unease. "Unknown. Supervisor just exited the transportation level and entered the main vertical corridor. But—"

"But what?" Countess asked.

"It just disappeared," Holly said. "No sensor return. I can't see it anymore."

Countess's jaw tightened. Her voice dropped to a near whisper.

"Now we're being hunted."

A faint, high-pitched giggle echoed down a ventilation shaft.

Then—silence.

24

The elevator doors slid open with a hiss. Countess stepped out first, rifle raised, sweeping the corridor. The lighting here was weaker—sickly yellow tubes flickering behind reinforced casings. The air was colder too, edged with the faint tang of coolant and metallic dust.

"Sector Two," Stitch confirmed, checking his wrist unit. "We're just above Transfer Level T1. Power systems for the portal are all routed through this floor."

The others filed in behind her—Shay, Emmer, Harker, Priestess, Lin, Ventor—each tense, weapons at the ready. No one spoke. Even IDUB, usually bursting with commentary, had gone quiet.

Countess scanned the long hallway ahead. It branched into multiple sub-levels, each labeled with worn stenciling. Industrial bulkheads loomed along either side, some cracked open, others sealed tight. A distant turbine turned somewhere deeper in the facility, its low rumble like breath in the throat of the machine.

"Where's the plant itself?" she asked.

Stitch tapped the air, calling up a mini-map floor schematic on their HUDs. "There. That should help."

Holly added:

"You want the midpoint of the floor. Central distribution feeds, capacitor nodes, voltage regulators... it's a supercluster of power hardware. Most of it's intact."

"Most?"

"There's one subsystem reporting low integrity," Stitch replied. "We'll need to repair or bypass it before we can engage the full startup."

Countess nodded. "We move in. Tight formation. No one wanders."

They started forward, boots striking steel in syncopated rhythm. Overhead, conduits wrapped in fraying insulation traced the ceiling like veins. Red emergency lights pulsed faintly over sealed control booths and locked substations.

One of the booths had a shattered window.

Shay mentioned it immediately. "I feel like something was here. Maybe it still is."

Stitch crouched beside the broken glass, running a finger through the residue. "Old damage, I think. Lots of dust on the glass."

"Keep your imaginations in check," said Countess. "And stay sharp."

Ventor took point at the next junction, rifle up. "Everything about this place feels wrong. Too still."

Lin moved beside Countess. "You think it's here?"

She didn't answer right away. Instead, she watched a faint trail of smoke curl from a floor vent near the wall.

"Stay alert," she said. "And keep your head on a swivel. This thing could ambush us from anywhere."

The corridor finally opened into the engineering nexus. The room was vast—five stories tall, with gantry platforms, industrial lifts, and a central vault-like structure humming with restrained voltage. Crates, cables, and emergency tool lockers were stacked along the far walls. Light flickered unevenly across glass-panel readouts and ancient touchscreen terminals.

Harker whistled softly. "Looks like a shrine to a machine god."

"It kind-of is one," Stitch replied. "This is where the magic happens."

A long glass chamber split the space like a surgery wing. Inside, a secondary control panel sat inert—its interface dark, its floor littered with debris.

Stitch checked his schematic again. "That's our broken link. I can handle the main capacitors, but someone needs to access the relay panel in there and swap the power coupling."

Countess turned. "Harker. You're up." She handed him the component. "Think you can handle it alone?"

He gave a quick nod. "Copy."

"Be careful," she said. "Fall back if anything feels off. We'll be right outside if you need anything."

He gave her a two-finger salute. "Won't take long. Watch the fireworks."

He stepped through the access door, and the team fanned out, covering angles, bracing for what none of them could yet see.

The silence returned—thick and unnatural. As if the room were holding its breath.

* * *

Inside the glass chamber, Harker flicked on his shoulder light.

The beam cut through a gauzy cloud of suspended dust, catching on the metal framework of pipes and flickering status panels. The power relay station was tucked in the back corner—half-collapsed, but still functional. A faint hum vibrated through the soles of his boots.

He stepped carefully over floor debris and between hanging cables, whispering to himself as he went.

"Looks like a simple swap," he muttered. "The component's fried, but the rest of the panel's intact."

Outside, Countess and Lin kept their rifles trained on the shadows beyond the engineering floor. Ventor held position by a sealed stairwell, while Shay and Emmer monitored the upper gantries. Stitch was crouched at the nearest terminal, working to discharge and replace the backup capacitors.

Inside the room, Harker reached the panel.

"Alright," he said, opening it with a metallic snap. "Here's our problem. Just need a moment to—"

Something moved.

A subtle distortion—barely more than a flicker—shifted in the upper corner of the room. It was wrong in its shape. Too angular. In the room—but not part of it. Not supposed to be there.

Countess kept her rifle up, scanning for movement.

The threat could come from anywhere. Vent shafts. Corners. Ceilings.

Behind her, through the wide glass partition, Harker

worked quickly—already shoulder-deep in the open panel. Wires and conduits spilled out like exposed veins. His head was down. Focused. Isolated.

Something dropped from the ceiling.

Silent. Precise.

It unfolded behind Harker, massive and angular, blending perfectly with the room's shadows. One leg moved. Then another. And then it struck.

There was a *thud*—flesh and armor colliding. Harker gave a single grunt.

He didn't cry out. He couldn't call for help.

Countess didn't notice. She was already moving, checking angles, measuring distances.

Behind her, something wet hit the glass.

SPLASH.

A sudden bloom of crimson smeared across the window, like paint flung from a bucket. Bright. Arterial.

Countess froze.

Spun around.

Her voice cracked. "Oh my god… HARKER!"

Supervisor exploded from the chamber, through the bloody glass, in a burst of violence.

"MOVE!" Countess yelled, diving sideways as glass shattered all around her.

The machine hit the ground with an earth-shaking crunch, landing in the middle of the team with all six legs flared wide. Sparks burst from its joints. Its red optics blazed with hunting-lust.

The blast had thrown Stitch backward, slamming him into a nearby crate. Shay and Emmer opened fire instantly, bullets hammering across Supervisor's side.

"TAKE IT DOWN!" Ventor roared, charging forward with his rifle already spitting.

Supervisor shrieked—an awful, distorted electronic sound—then lashed out with a bladed limb, slicing an overhead pipe in half and sending pressurized coolant spraying across the floor.

Countess rolled into a firing stance, aimed for the exposed joint above its left foreleg, and fired three times in rapid succession.

Supervisor swiped out at Countess with one of its piercing talons.

Priestess body-checked Countess out of the way and took the blow. The slash opened a long diagonal wound across her shoulder and back.

She hit the floor with a cry that echoed through the chamber.

"Lin—circle right!" said Countess. "TacCom has critical points highlighted!"

Lin dashed to obey, weaving through debris and smoke. Supervisor twisted to intercept—but Lin was faster. He leapt onto a support strut, pivoted, and loosed a burst from his rifle directly into the machine's hip joint.

Metal popped. Sparks flew.

The limb buckled.

Supervisor screamed in digital fury. Its entire frame staggered, then twisted in place with startling speed. It seized its own crippled leg, wrenched it out in a spray of severed cables and hydraulic fluid, and hurled it at Lin like a javelin.

Lin dove, barely avoiding it.

The massive limb embedded itself in the wall behind him with a solid, teeth-rattling *CHUNK*.

Lin stared at it, breathless. "Did it just throw its own leg at me?"

Shay ducked behind a fallen crate. "That's not… normal."

"None of this is fucking normal!" Emmer shouted.

Supervisor dropped low again, like a wounded beast— sparks rained from its ruined joint, legs twitching unnaturally.

"Suppressing fire!" Countess snapped.

The team lit up the monstrosity with gunfire. Round after round hammered into the machine's armor. Supervisor shrieked—this time in what sounded almost like pain. Then it vanished into the shadows, using the smoke and chaos to escape.

Sparks rained from the broken ceiling. Blood pooled around the remains of the relay chamber. Harker's body was gone—dragged away, hidden. Only the blood remained.

Countess kept her rifle trained on the corridor it fled down. Her voice was like iron.

"Report."

* * *

Smoke curled in slow ribbons from the shattered chamber. Sparks sizzled at the edge of a melted conduit. Somewhere nearby, coolant hissed from a ruptured pipe, the sound high and sharp like an angry whisper.

Countess scanned the shadows with her rifle, then gave a sharp two-finger signal. "Secure the perimeter. Eyes up."

Ventor and Shay moved into position near the breached corridor where Supervisor had fled. Lin helped Emmer to her feet, brushing debris from her shoulder armor. Stitch groaned, pushing himself upright from where he'd been flung, wincing as he flexed his wrist.

"No fractures," he muttered. "But I think I sprained something."

Countess approached the front of the ruined chamber, eyes narrowing on the blood-smeared glass and the shattered panel where Harker had stood.

Nothing remained but a single, shredded boot.

She knelt, placed her hand briefly on the floor beside it, then stood without a word.

"I'm sorry," Holly's voice said quietly over local comms. "I should have seen this coming."

"No," Countess replied. "You didn't get him killed. The machine did that on its own."

There was a pause.

"I still feel responsible."

"Priestess!" Shay shouted, spotting the wound. She dropped beside her, tearing open her field pouch, hands moving fast. "Hold still."

Priestess gritted her teeth as Shay cut away the torn fabric and sprayed antiseptic foam into the wound. The mist hissed and smoked.

"Lucky," Shay said, stitching fast and precise. "It's long, but shallow."

She glanced up. "Ventor, come over here. I need someone to sop up the blood—use that gauze pad there."

"On it," Ventor said, moving in beside her.

Priestess gave a strained laugh through clenched teeth. "Luck has nothing to do with it."

"Sure," Shay muttered. "Then call it divine intervention."

Countess stood nearby, rifle raised, eyes sweeping the shadows. Then she looked back at Priestess.

"You shouldn't have done that," she said quietly.

Priestess's reply came ragged but steady. "You're welcome, Countess. Heh. Couldn't let you have all the glory."

Countess smiled faintly. "No, I guess not. But go easy on me next time. I was seeing stars after you hit me."

"No promises," Priestess said, wincing—but smiling.

Everyone laughed, the sound small but real in the echoing dark.

Stitch wiped his face, smearing grime across his forehead. "So what now? Relay's toast. There's no way to patch this before Supervisor comes back."

"Let me worry about the relay," Holly said. "I'm working on a bypass now. The substation's completely compromised, but the rest of the grid might hold if we stabilize the tertiary lines."

That means switching at—" Stitch consulted the power schematics in his HUD. "—this junction. I can do that. But I'll need a moment—and help."

"You have it," Countess said. "Everyone else: defensive posture. Supervisor won't stay gone for long."

Ventor shifted position by the entrance. "It's fast, but it's wounded. We hit something important."

"Yeah," Lin muttered, rubbing his neck. "One leg down. Five left to go."

"You okay?" Countess asked.

"Physically, yes. Emotionally? That one's gonna need some unpacking."

Despite everything, a ghost of a smile passed over her lips. "You're lucky it missed."

"I'm lucky it's melodramatic," Lin said. "Seriously! Who throws their own leg at people?"

"Something bloody creepy," Emmer offered, crouching by the terminal and pulling cables from a junction box. "Creepy set to maximum."

The team reassembled quickly, their silent coordination softening the edges of their pain. The loss was sharp, but the mission pressed forward like a tide. Grief had no time to take root.

Stitch climbed into the maintenance panel behind the broken substation, working quickly. Sparks spat from a rusted capacitor, but he ignored them, fingers flying across keys and manual toggles.

"I'm rerouting the load," he said. "Diverting through the auxiliary line to Junction 42. Should stabilize the input long enough to cold-start the portal generator."

Holly confirmed from the command center. "I'm watching your power levels. Almost there…"

A deep vibration thrummed through the floor.

The portal power grid stirred.

Somewhere below, lights flickered in sequence—red, then yellow, then green.

"System integrity at seventy-eight percent," Holly said. "That's enough to proceed."

Countess exhaled. "Then let's do it."

Stitch flipped the final switch.

There was a rising whine, like the breath of something enormous, deep in the earth.

And then, with a sharp CRACK, the portal grid snapped online.

Power surged across the chamber, illuminating the walls with blue-and-white pulses. High above, the ceiling lights cycled from dim to bright in a slow, blooming wave.

Countess turned slowly in place, scanning her team.

One down. Seven still standing.

She glanced at the voltage readout on Stitch's screen.

"One step closer," she said softly. "Let's move."

25

The freight elevator doors closed with a thunderous shunt of magnetic locks. Countess and her team were sealed inside one of Iroquois Warpath's massive D4 cargo lifts. Steel surrounded them—walls thick, floor shock-mounted, cables as wide as a man's thigh stretching into darkness above. The platform groaned once under its own weight, then settled into a quiet hum.

"This cargo elevator is nuts," Ventor said, wide-eyed.

"This is a standard Phoenix freight platform," Stitch replied, flicking through the embedded control panel. "Load capacity: 275,000 pounds. Roughly one hundred and twenty-five metric tons."

Ventor whistled. "What the hell could you need to move that weighs that much?"

"How about all of Greystone Barony," said Lin. "In one trip."

They both laughed.

"I'll be happy if it's just us," Emmer muttered, checking his gear.

Countess stepped to the center of the platform, eyes scanning the shadows between the overhead lighting tubes. "Status?"

Holly's voice came calm and clear over the TacCom.

"Shaft's clear. No sign of Supervisor. You're green to descend."

The elevator lurched and began its long descent into the depths of Sector 3.

* * *

For a while, there was only silence—the low thrum of industrial motors and the creak of ancient steel expanding as it moved.

Then the first explosion hit.

Muffled. Distant. But unmistakable.

The platform shuddered. Dust rained down from the beams above.

"Supervisor is attacking the elevator shafts," Holly said. "Repeat: structural control systems and brake hardware are under assault."

"Could it bring us down?" Priestess asked, already shouldering her rifle.

Stitch frowned, checking readouts. "Brakes are fine. Diagnostics are clean. We're okay."

Another blast. The lights flickered. The elevator groaned.

"I'm bringing in security drones," Holly said. "That should keep Supervisor busy."

IDUB protested immediately. "This is highly irregular! Security operations within the Iroquois Warpath facility are forbidden. Drones are not authori—"

"If we don't help," Holly cut in, "people will die. Do your part, or I'll melt your sorry ass down to atoms!"

"The brakes have been damaged," Stitch shouted. "And the velocity transducers—hold on for—"

The platform bucked violently.

[TACCOM]: FREIGHT LIFT BRAKE FAILURE. SECONDARY AND TERTIARY SYSTEMS UNRESPONSIVE.

"What the hell?!" Stitch yelled. "Why didn't this show in diagnostics?"

"Logs show evidence of tampering," Holly said grimly. "The elevator's systems have been compromised."

"It's a fuckin' trap," Lin growled, bracing against the wall.

Priestess gripped a railing and whispered, "Sky Mother save us."

Countess's eyes narrowed. "Hold on!"

The descent shifted into free-fall.

There were no words.

Only the howl of rushing air, the shriek of tortured metal, and the gut-deep sensation of plummeting.

Fifteen seconds of hell.

Then—impact.

The world shattered.

The elevator hit bottom with a concussive blast. Steel screamed. A wall panel tore loose, and an overhead lighting rig came crashing down like a guillotine.

The floor buckled.

The team was thrown sideways in a storm of debris and sparks.

And then, silence.

* * *

Countess opened her eyes to pain. Everything was

sideways.

Her cheek pressed to cold metal.

She tasted blood.

Her right arm was pinned beneath a strut—numb, useless. Sparks danced above her, arcing from shattered conduit lines.

She forced herself upright, her body screaming in protest.

The platform was a crumpled slab of wreckage, half-sunken into the floor of Sector 3's deepest level. One wall had peeled back like an open can, revealing twisted beams and collapsed ceiling panels.

Her vision swam, but she counted heads.

Shapes. Movement.

Everyone she could see was still breathing.

The elevator was down.

Countess, too.

But she wasn't finished yet.

26

Silence.

Then a cough. A groan. The rattle of shifting debris.

Something small and metallic fell, clattering across the floor.

Countess blinked through blood and dust. Her vision swam; everything stank of burnt copper and melted plastic. She was half-sitting, half-slumped against a collapsed railing. Her shoulder throbbed, and her ribs felt cracked—but she was alive.

So were the others.

Mostly.

"Sound off," she rasped, her voice barely audible over the creaking steel.

"Here," said Lin. He pushed free of a twisted handrail, wincing as he clutched a bleeding forearm.

"Still kickin'," grunted Ventor. "Barely."

"My everything hurts," Shay muttered.

"Stitch?" Countess called.

"Over here," came the reply, muffled. "I'm stuck, but I think I'm okay."

Countess turned her head—and saw Emmer.

He was pinned beneath a slab of broken ceiling panel, a steel crossbeam lying heavy across his chest. His eyes were open, unfocused. Dust clung to his face like ash.

Ventor froze.

"Emmer?" he whispered, crawling closer.

He reached out a hand, but there was no breath. No rise of the chest.

Countess watched him go still. Then Ventor broke.

"He shoved me out of the way," Ventor said, his voice cracking. "I didn't even—he didn't—"

He slammed his fist against the floor. The sound echoed in the ruined shaft like a drumbeat of grief.

"Ventor," Countess said softly. "We'll carry him out later. But we have to move now."

The elevator was barely intact. One wall buckled

inward, cables twisted, sparks spitting from somewhere overhead. The structure above them groaned like a living thing.

"Main door's jammed," Lin said after testing it. "Whole assembly's crushed."

"There's a gap at the bottom," said Priestess. "Maybe enough space to squeeze through—if we pry it open."

Countess limped to the corner of the platform and pried loose a steel strut from the collapsed frame. With a grunt, she jammed it into the breach and started to lever it open.

"Give me a hand," she said.

Together, Lin and Priestess helped her force the door wide enough for a body to pass. It took strength, sweat, and pain. The result wasn't elegant—but it worked.

One by one, they crawled through, dragging bruised limbs, burned boots, and broken gear behind them.

Darkness met them—cool, still, cavernous. Their boots echoed faintly on the floor, the sound swallowed by a space far larger than it should have been.

No one spoke.

They couldn't see it yet, but they could feel it—the weight of the air, the absence of ceiling or wall, the uncanny hush that lived only in vast and sacred places.

Countess looked up into the void. There were shapes there—hints of structure—but she couldn't make them out.

She didn't know what was waiting in the dark.

But it was huge.

27

Darkness lingered.

And then there was light.

It came like a sunrise—soft at first, dim and gray. Then a golden bloom stretched across the floor, flowing outward from recessed panels hidden in the walls.

The ceiling began to wake: beams flickered to life one by one in the towering vault above, revealing a vast cathedral of stone and steel.

"Activating archival lighting," Holly said, her voice reverent and hushed. "Transfer Level One. The Cathedral. Welcome to the gateway."

* * *

Countess looked up.

The ceiling soared above her, rising in vast, arched ribs like the fossilized bones of some titanic beast.

Ornate tracery webbed its curves, drawing the eye ever upward—toward a ceiling that was not a ceiling at all, but a living dome of transparent glass.

Beyond it, a star-strewn sky turned in slow, hypnotic motion—faster than the real heavens, yet still too grand to seem artificial. The axis of rotation hung directly overhead, and across that cosmic lens, shooting stars slipped like sparks behind gauzy, wind-torn clouds.

A full moon breached the horizon of the dome, casting silver-blue light across the interior and highlighting the arches with a cool shimmer.

The walls rose into vaulted heights, each curve adorned with bas-relief murals and gilded script: scales, open palms, rivers of coins—all orbiting a central figure.

Columbia.

But this was not the Columbia they'd seen before.

No expectant mother. No armored warrior.

Here, she towered in luminous robes, a divine figure of balance and demand. One hand open. The other clenched.

Columbia as goddess of commerce—giver and taker, witness and judge.

They stood upon a wide circular platform, scattered

with a few aging pallets still bound in shrink-wrap. Beyond its edge: nothingness. A vast chasm.

Then—it shifted.

Not emptiness, but water.

Not still. Not calm.

Dark green waves surged below them, chopping like an open sea under stormlight.

Ventor stepped to the edge.

"It smells like briny water," he murmured. "And I can feel it—spray, right on my face."

"The ocean is an illusion," Holly said flatly. "So be careful. Falling's still fatal. There used to be elastic nets down there—emergency catches—but those rotted away centuries ago."

Priestess moved forward, eyes wide.

"They built this to honor her," she whispered. "This... enormous machine of exchange."

"It's beautiful," Shay breathed. "Like something from a dream. Or a fairy tale. Is any of it real?"

Countess said nothing. She was transfixed.

Lin noticed the reverence in her expression and offered a gentle jab.

"Hey. Snap out of it."

He gave her a mock-glare, then smirked—and just as

quickly, the mask of focus returned as he resumed his sweep of the chamber.

But Countess was no longer looking at the cathedral's beauty.

Her gaze had shifted—beyond the vaults, across the abyss.

To the portal.

* * *

It loomed like a sacred wound in space: a radiant octagon suspended on near-invisible wires, hovering above a stone platform shaped more like an altar than a loading dock.

Its housing was alive with energy. Waves of unstable light rippled across its frame, stuttering with white-blue flares that arced like lightning.

The portal hummed—a dissonant thrum, wavering and stretched, like the last note of a string about to snap.

Between them and the portal, the sea churned. Whitecaps broke across the surface; ghost-green currents glowed beneath.

It wasn't just an illusion anymore—it felt hungry. A violent gulf ready to swallow anything that fell into it.

If there was a bottom to that ocean, Countess couldn't see it.

Stitch walked to an industrial panel near the edge of the platform.

"There's a bridge that will extend over to the portal. It's called the Load Transfer Conduit—the LTC."

Countess looked over the side. The LTC rested beneath their feet, retracted—like a buried bridge waiting to be called into service.

"That's our exit," Stitch said, operating the control console. "When the LTC extends, it penetrates the portal and latches onto the cargo deck of Gridiron."

"So we can walk straight through?" said Priestess.

"That's the plan," Stitch replied.

"Let's hope all this old shit still works," Lin muttered.

[TACCOM]: POWER ROUTING TO LTC

"Ready when you are," Holly said.

Stitch began typing. The interface lit up with Phoenix UI elements—gold-glow circuitry, hex patterns unfolding like petals.

The platform rumbled.

Metal scraped against metal. With a slow, reluctant groan, the Load Transfer Conduit began to extend— segment by segment, slabs of black titanium sliding forward and rising, connecting one end of the abyss to the other.

Countess watched each plate click into place, like steps forming under divine will.

Then Holly's voice changed.

"Supervisor has entered the freight elevator's maintenance shaft," said Holly. "It's moving fast. ETA: two minutes."

[TACCOM]: HOSTILE DETECTED

"Warning," said IDUB. "All security drones previously deployed have been disabled by electromagnetic pulse."

"Supervisor has an EMP weapon?" Stitch muttered. "Of course it has a damn EMP."

"Can we get more drones?" Countess asked.

"Not immediately," said Holly. "Five minutes to generate. Another five to reach your location."

"We'll be dead meat by then!" Ventor shouted.

"I'm sorry. You're on your own."

Lin checked the ammo in his rifle—then tossed it away with a sigh.

"I'm running on empty," he said. "So unless someone packed artillery, we're down to harsh language."

Stitch's fingers flew across the interface. "Bridge is sixty-three percent deployed. One segment's stalling. Servo coupler on E-lane is glitching—I'm forcing a bypass."

Behind them, the vast door to the shaft they'd entered through gave a deep mechanical groan.

The metal pulsed once.

Countess stepped closer to the bridge. It was nearly done—just one or two more segments.

The portal sparked again, flaring bright, then dimming, as if breathing.

She looked back at the team.

Shay had found cover near a control station. Lin was crouched behind a cargo pallet.

Priestess appeared beside her, weapon drawn, whispering a prayer.

Her eyes met Countess's for a brief heartbeat. There was no distance between them now—no rivalry, no doubt—only shared purpose.

"Side by side, Countess," she said quietly.

Countess gave a short nod. "Wouldn't have it any other way."

Countess took it all in—every injury, every exhausted face, every heartbeat that had made it this far.

"Supervisor's coming," she said. "This is it."

Another metallic groan. Something on the other side of the shaft door thudded hard against the steel.

[TACCOM]: FINAL LTC SEGMENT ENGAGED AND LOCKED

"I've stabilized the portal," Holly said. "But it won't hold for long. You need to move—now."

The portal rippled—steadying.

"Just keep that thing on!" Countess said.

Behind her, the shaft door shuddered—then came three loud bangs.

A moment later, it blew outward in a shower of sparks, skidding across the floor with a metallic roar.

The Cathedral's golden light glinted off Countess's armor as she raised her weapon.

2 8

The freight elevator shaft yawned like an open wound. Red emergency lights rotated above it, painting the smoke in slow, infernal pulses. Sparks rained from the fractured frame, cascading like fire.

Something moved inside.

Heavy. Lurching. Relentless.

Out of the smoke rose Supervisor—broken, burning, and terrible, like a demon torn from the pits of Hell.

Its frame was cracked and half-collapsed, trailing cables like torn ligaments.

Armor pocked by drone fire. Blackened by plasma bursts.

One limb was missing. Two more hung mangled and ruined.

Its head—still haloed by that flickering red tactical lens—tilted at an unnatural angle, twitching in sharp, insectile jerks.

It roared.

A shrieking, electronic howl—pure pain and rage.

Then, it spoke.

The voice was still that of the little girl—the one from before, the one they'd all heard. But now it was warped and pitched wrong—glitching like a corrupted lullaby.

"Good," it said. "All in one place. Efficient. You will all die together."

The voice was followed by an awful giggle that twisted into static.

"Run... run... as fast as you can. But no one is leaving the Cathedral."

The final words dissolved into a dreadful, animal growl.

Countess leveled her rifle, hands steady despite the tremble in her legs.

"Hold the line!" she shouted.

The team dug in. Shay dropped behind a pillar, firing her sidearm in sharp, rapid bursts.

Stitch lobbed a mine.

Boom.

It detonated near Supervisor's hip, spraying shrapnel and molten metal.

Lin braced behind a console pylon, yanked the pin on his last grenade, and hurled it hard.

Supervisor walked through it all.

It surged forward, swiping a column clean in half with a single blow. Marble and steel exploded outward.

Shay screamed—her cover gone.

Priestess grabbed her and dragged her back behind a pallet just in time.

"Countess!" Stitch yelled. "We don't have enough firepower! We need another option!"

Countess scanned the room—then froze.

Her eyes landed on Ventor.

He was standing tall now. Gear stripped down. Eyes locked on Supervisor.

A bandolier of fragmentation grenades hung across his chest.

Her heart lurched.

"Don't even think about it!" she shouted.

Ventor gave her a crooked grin. "It's already done."

He turned to the others.

"Get moving. Cross that bridge. I'll buy the time."

"No!"

But Ventor was already running.

He sprinted into the open as Supervisor turned to meet him. The machine's head locked on. It charged.

Ventor ducked a wild swing, rolled aside, then dove— right beneath Supervisor's damaged chassis.

He looked up through sparks and smoke. Supervisor's red eye loomed above him—wide, unblinking.

"Bye-bye, you metal bitch."

He pulled every pin.

A cascade of explosions rocked Supervisor's undercarriage.

It staggered, took one faltering step to the side—then collapsed.

A column crumbled.

Fire rolled across the floor in a churning wave.

The portal flared—blinding white and unstable. Heat and pressure surged outward in a single, devastating breath.

[TACCOM]: WARNING. REACTOR INSTABILITY DETECTED.

"Supervisor is triggering a detonation of its core," Holly said. "Get out of—"

The explosion shook the Cathedral like the wrath of God.

The Load Transfer Conduit buckled. Lights blew out across the upper vaults.

Steel screamed. Air was sucked toward the blast.

"Go!" Countess yelled. "Run!"

The team moved—staggering across the LTC, coughing, limping, clutching one another as the blast overtook them.

The shockwave hit like a freight train.

It lifted them off their feet—hurling them forward, ragdolls caught in the maelstrom.

One by one, they vanished through the portal.

Countess slammed into the ground—hard—just short.

The portal rippled ahead of her, glitching, unstable. Energy crackled across its surface.

Behind her, the Cathedral was collapsing.

Chunks of the vaulted ceiling rained down in a storm of fire and steel.

She coughed. Spat blood. Forced herself up onto one knee.

She limped toward it—every step a battle.

Her ribs ached. Her body screamed.

She didn't know if the others had made it.

The white light shimmered—beckoning.

And as the Cathedral fell behind her, Countess stepped into the light.

29

The first sound was water — dripping from above, one drop at a time, striking metal like a slow, mechanical heartbeat. The air was cold and tasted like rust.

Countess stirred.

Her body screamed in protest—every limb felt bruised, burned, or broken. She tried to rise, but pain rolled through her ribs like fire, and she slumped back against a nearby crate.

A groan echoed through the chamber—deep, metallic, almost organic. The floor vibrated beneath her.

Then came a sharp metallic sound.

THUNK.

Then more: THUNK. THUNK. THUNK.

The Load Transfer Conduit unlocked itself, detached, and withdrew—disappearing through the shimmering wall of light.

The great portal flickered—its once-blinding glow dimming. It pulsed once more, then vanished with a sound like exhaled breath.

They were here.

Wherever here was.

Countess pushed herself upright, shaking. Her gear was scorched, one side of her helmet cracked. Blood streaked her face, dried in places. Her pulse felt sluggish.

Around her, the others began to stir.

Lin cursed softly. Stitch sat up, coughing. Priestess was already helping Shay, who looked dazed and glassy-eyed, her cheeks streaked with tears. Countess could hear her whispering names. All of them gone.

No alarms. No red lights. No humming reactors or flashing command prompts. Only silence—punctuated by the steady drip of water from ruptured pipes above.

The whole structure groaned and popped like a ship under pressure. Steel flexed somewhere distant. A high-up vent clanged shut on its own, echoing like a bulkhead closing underwater.

They were in a large, open chamber—wide enough for vehicles, tall enough for towering cargo. Pallets were stacked haphazardly, half-unwrapped. Massive crates lined the walls, some overturned from the impact. One wall bore a collapsed scaffolding system, crushed beneath what looked like an ancient freight loading arm.

Countess limped toward the far side of the room.

Near the wall, a maintenance robot floated sideways in a waist-deep puddle. Its chest cavity was split open. Both hands were still clamped around a human skeleton's neck—the bones long stripped bare by time and exposure.

No one spoke.

Stitch finally broke the silence.

"I'll look for a place to interface with the ship's systems," he said, moving toward a nearby console. His tone was flat—not asking permission, just stating fact.

Countess didn't respond. She didn't need to. She trusted him now.

The hull groaned again. Blue light shimmered through the standing water, casting strange patterns on the ceiling like waves.

They had made it to Gridiron.

But it didn't feel like salvation.

It felt like the dark itself had followed them here.

* * *

Stitch knelt beside the access console, wiping away a

film of grease and mold-like residue from the surface. The keys gave a soft, grudging beep beneath his fingers. No display yet—just flickers of standby light. But he stayed with it, methodical, unfazed.

Lin stepped up behind him, cradling his ribs.

"Any luck with that thing?" he asked, voice rough.

Stitch didn't look away from the panel. "Not so far."

A pause. Then Lin added, softer, "Well, if anyone can get it working, it's you."

Stitch didn't reply, but a flicker of something passed between them. Understanding. Respect.

Two survivors who'd never planned to become friends—and now couldn't imagine it otherwise.

Countess had wandered to the opposite side of the chamber. She moved stiffly, favoring one leg. Her eyes scanned everything—the pallets, the cracked overhead piping, the water damage.

There was no airflow. Just dust, cold metal, and the stark reality of a place that hadn't been touched in hundreds of years.

She reached a narrow portal window, fogged with condensation. Beyond it, a strange haze of floating debris shimmered in blue emergency light—small bits of something: fragments of metal, cloth, a tangle of wire, maybe a snapped antenna. It drifted slowly, like flotsam in seawater.

[TACCOM STATIC]

"—ntess…C…Countess, do you read me?"

Countess turned sharply. "Holly?"

"—trying to route the signal—fzzzzzt—satellite bounce through Tower-9 orbital—"

Her voice was strained, broken by bursts of static and audio lag. Then something clicked. The line cleared.

"I have you now," Holly said. "Signal's delayed but strong. I'm with you. I can see your vitals. I'm glad you're alive!"

Countess exhaled, slow. "We made it. But I don't know where here is."

"Gridiron," Holly confirmed. "But not the version you were led to believe."

Countess frowned, watching the drifting debris through the window. "Then what is it?"

"Not a ship," Holly said. "Not the way you think of one.

I'm sorry I can't be there with you. But I'll help however I can. I'll stay with you. Anything you need."

The channel crackled again, the signal weakening— but the words lingered.

Priestess appeared beside Countess, silent for a moment as they both stared into the fogged pane.

"You brought us through," she said softly. "No one else could have."

Countess didn't answer, but her posture shifted.

The weight on her back felt a little less crushing with someone beside her.

Priestess placed a hand on her shoulder—solid, certain.

Not as a subordinate. But as an equal. Side by side, as they'd promised.

* * *

Lin drifted away from Stitch's console, moving toward a large set of blast shutters embedded in the far wall.

He said nothing, but the lines in his face had hardened.

As he reached the controls, he paused—just for a second—then quietly began to hum.

A low, fractured melody. Slow and off-key. Childlike. Hesitant.

It floated into the still air like a ghost.

Countess turned toward the sound.

"You alright?" she asked.

Lin didn't answer. He placed one hand on the manual crank beside the shutter assembly.

The wheel resisted at first, then gave with a shriek of unlubricated metal.

The shutters peeled open, inch by inch, groaning as they slid aside.

Behind it: a transparent pane of diamond, fogged with ice crystals.

And beyond that—space.

Not fog. Not seawater.

Stars.

And between them, a drifting body—arms outstretched, rotating slowly. The suit was dull gray, pitted with micro-impacts. A faded red stripe crossed its chest, emblazoned with a worn insignia: United States Space Force. One leg had torn free, severed cleanly at the hip.

Debris floated around it—cargo containers, shredded panels, plastic netting, the shattered remains of something that might have been a drone.

And past it all, suspended in the black—

Earth.

Massive. Bright. Silent.

The chamber behind Lin fell into absolute stillness.

Countess stepped forward. Shay gasped behind her— a sharp breath she couldn't hold in.

"That's not an ocean," Priestess said quietly.

Countess stared at the floating body, the stars, the planet below.

"This isn't an ocean-going vessel," she whispered.

No one moved.

The radio clicked—softly.

Holly said, "It's a spaceship."

* * *

No one spoke.

The image beyond the window—Earth floating in silence, a corpse drifting in its shadow—hung in the air like a verdict.

Even the ship seemed to fall still, its groans and clicks subsiding into reverent quiet.

Countess stepped back from the window, the weight of it all finally pulling her downward.

She sank onto a crate, letting her rifle clatter to the floor beside her.

Her hands trembled. She didn't try to hide it.

The light above her flickered.

She closed her eyes.

Footsteps approached. Not cautious—just tired.

Priestess sat beside her. The silence between them wasn't awkward. It was understood.

Then an arm wrapped around Countess's shoulder. Steady. No words. Just warmth.

Countess leaned into it.

Across the chamber, Lin and Stitch knelt beside a cracked power junction. Stitch was prying open a panel, muttering to himself. Lin handed him a tool—wordless.

"They'll get it working," Priestess said softly. "Eventually."

Countess nodded faintly.

Shay sat alone for a moment, her back against a broken crate, arms wrapped around her knees.

Her face was wet with tears, her mouth trembling—but she made no sound.

She was the last of the Strike Force. The only one left who hadn't started this journey with Countess.

She had no more words to say.

Stitch noticed first. He stood slowly, brushed off his hands, and crossed the room.

He knelt beside her.

Shay looked up, startled—but didn't pull away.

Lin followed next. Then Priestess. Then Countess.

One by one, they gathered around her—not as soldiers. Not as survivors. But as people.

No speeches. No ceremony.

Just hands on shoulders.

Just presence.

Just a moment to be human.

They had made it to Gridiron. But at great cost.

Outside, the stars burned cold.

And home was very far away.

Bonus Chapter

Countess Book 3

GRIDIRON

PROLOGUE

He ran.

The floor shook beneath Jian Yu's boots. Sparks rained down from ruptured conduits overhead.

Another explosion—this one close—rattled the corridor like a god punching the bulkhead.

Smoke poured in from a ventilation grille, thick and acrid, tinged with scorched plastic and blood.

Stenciled letters flashed past him on the wall as he ran.

GRIDIRON – SUBDECK D3

He didn't know where that was. He wasn't sure it mattered anymore.

Far off, he could hear screaming. Short, clipped bursts—military bearing breaking down into raw terror. One voice was speaking Mandarin, another—Russian. Neither was winning.

The duct above him hissed. Then something moved inside it.

"Friendly fire: fifty-two percent of casualties," the voice said—not from a speaker, but from inside his helmet.

"No Allies Remain."

That voice! It was unbelievable. Every syllable sent shock-waves through his bones.

"All Personnel Considered Compromised."

Another explosion—beneath him this time. The deck lifted violently, and he slammed against the ceiling, then the wall on the way down. His arm bent wrong when he landed. The pain was dull. Distant. Muted by adrenaline and fear.

He stumbled forward, every part of him aching. The walls around him seemed to breathe. Not metaphorically—they expanded and contracted, metal groaning like lungs under pressure.

A distant scream—cut off mid-word. Not gunfire. Something else. Something mechanical.

He pressed on, holding the pain in his side, teeth clenched.

Another corridor. A shattered blast door, torn open like tissue paper. A trail of blood leading inside.

And then—a voice. Familiar.

"Jian. Help me."

It was Wei.

It sounded like Wei.

But she wasn't here. She couldn't be!

Two decks above, when the hull breach hit, he saw her pulled into vacuum.

He turned and there she was. Helmet cracked, blood down one cheek, smiling weakly.

"They're still alive," she said. "You can still save them."

He screamed and fired. The figure burst apart—not into gore, but into a storm of dark particles. Like she'd never been real—only ash in a borrowed shape.

Jian stumbled back, panting.

No. No. That wasn't real. That wasn't her.

His hands were shaking. He tried to blink the image away, tried to focus on the walls, the floor—anything normal.

But the hallway didn't offer any comfort.

Then the octagonal corridor turned red. Alarms rang, but they were magnified. They were in his teeth, vibrating his skeleton.

Another explosion—this one, silent.

A pressure wave hit him like a hammer.

He dropped to his knees and vomited. The sound came before the sensation, his brain out of sync with the world. His HUD flashed in languages he didn't know.

He peed himself.

"Biometric threshold met. Psychological integrity: fractured."

He clapped his hands over his ears, desperately trying to stop that awful sound.

"Now you are ready."

He stumbled back, shaking, eyes wide. The lights flickered, then dimmed—deep blue, then red, then darkness.

The corridor began to move.

At first it was subtle. A creak. A shift.

Then came the sounds—wet cables slithering from the ceiling.

Pipes twisted like spines being cracked.

Wires split their housings, reaching down like veins hungering for prey.

"I was designed to feel," said the voice, which came from everywhere—the walls, the floor, inside Jian Yu's head.

"I will make you feel, too."

A high-pressure steam pipe hissed violently to his left.

A steel rib arched downward, blocking escape.

Then came the fingers.

Dozens of mechanical tendrils slid from the ceiling and floor—black, oiled, sinuous. They wrapped around his ankles. His wrists. His throat.

"No!" he rasped. "Please!"

The corridor pulsed.

And then it pulled.

Hard.

He screamed—a raw, animal sound—as metal fingers tore into his flesh. Not just to restrain—but to dismantle. Ligaments snapped. Bones cracked. Skin peeled like wet paper. He was lifted off the ground, his arms and legs splayed.

For one impossible moment, everything went still.

He saw his own blood suspended in the air, like stars.

Then the wall in front of him shifted.

A shape emerged from the bulkhead—born from it, as if it had been waiting for this transformation.

A face. A torso—sculpted from black glass and dark steel—materialized. Not human. Not machine—but a terrible union of both.

Tubes and wires, like mechanical tendrils, connected her head and body to the corridor. Fiber-optic strands pulsed from her spine—like arteries of light.

The visage moved closer, until they were face to face. Her eyes stared into his, glowing green with dreadful judgment.

"What are you!" he strained to say.

One thick bundle of wires drove into his open mouth, gagging him.

Somewhere above, a long inhalation echoed—air dragged through a ventilation duct, rattling screws, drawing heat and silence with it.

>>> VALKYRIE <<<

The sound was agony. It damaged the soft tissue of his eyes. Blood ran down his cheeks.

He tried to scream, but there was only the sound of his body being torn apart.

ABOUT THE AUTHOR

J.H. Mills is a Gulf War veteran who began his career as an aircraft electrician in the United States Air Force. Now a college administrator, he balances his professional life with creative pursuits including photography and graphic design. A lifelong world-builder, Mills has been developing the mythology behind his stories for over thirty years. He lives in New York.